SPARK & FIZZ BOOKS PRESENTS

PLANET SCUMM

AUTUMN 2022   "EXTINCTION EVENTS"   ISSUE NO. 14

— A DECORTICATED TABLE OF CONTENTS —

EDITOR-IN-CHIEF   CREATIVE DIRECTOR   MANAGING EDITOR   MARKETING DIRECTOR   PRODUCTION ARTIST
SEAN CLANCY   ALYSSA ALARCÓN SANTO   TYLER BERD   SAM RHEAUME   MAURA McGONAGLE

STAFF EDITOR   CONTENT STRATEGIST   COVER ART BY   SPOT ILLUSTRATIONS BY
ANNA CATALANO   LUCAS WISEMAN   KELLY WILLIAMS   MAURA McGONAGLE, SAM RHEAUME AND JORDAN ALARCON

S F
BOOKS

Planet Scumm is a triannual short fiction anthology. Visit **planetscumm.space** for submissions.

First Printing, 2022   ISBN: 978-1-970154-98-6

THE SCUMM INSTITUTE OF UNNATURAL HISTORY

Greetings, and welcome to the Scumm Institute of Unnatural History—the *only* history museum and research facility dedicated to alternate realities. I'm Smarty Scumm, and I'll be your guide today as we tour the exhibit hall and take a brief detour through our research offices. Stick close behind me for safety, and do please mind the slime.

The first exhibit on your left is *"Come the Banshee,"* by Maxine Sophia Wolff. The highlight of this collection is the funerary vessel—or "coffin"—you see on the center plinth there. There are competing theories among our team as to the exact meaning behind this vessel, but as you can see it does emit eels when approached.

I should have mentioned this earlier: if any of the exhibits here unexpectedly start to move or glow, your first instinct should be to close your mouth. Moving on!

"Single Malt Spacecraft," by Marie Vibbert, is a travelogue of sorts, chronicling one spacer's struggle with time-dilation and the potent potables she picked up along the way. We have a little tasting stand here that reproduces some of these drinks. Most of those samples should be well-aged and drinkable, but there may be a few that went a millenia too long in the barrel, so... fair warning.

In this next display, you'll recognize a familiar item: a simple jigsaw puzzle. This near-complete artifact, discovered by Frank Oreto and titled *"All Our Missing Pieces,"* was excavated from the ruins of a café in a neighboring reality. Quick note—if you happen to see a stray puzzle piece laying around as we continue on our tour, please leave it where it sits and *do not touch or try to complete the puzzle.* Or, if you cannot resist and *do* choose to complete it, grab a staff member first so we can take notes from a safe distance.

"Pharinexin," curated by Dale Stromberg, is a study on the divisive reality of rampant weapons proliferation, necessitated by the invention of a fast-acting, on-demand healing spray, which we have on display in that green spray canister there. Unfortunately, despite extensive testing, we've found that the item affords no such protection from the other exhibits here at the Scumm Institute.

By way of contrast, we have here our display for *"The Gardener"* by Logan A. Marrow. Digital records recovered from this reality suggest that a humble agricultural automaton may have, through some unknown means, developed an affinity for animal husbandry as well. Do avoid the sharp, rusty bits as you pass by—we haven't had a chance to install a safety barrier around this exhibit—and we also just think it looks cooler this way.

No, we haven't entered the cafeteria yet—this reproduction fish tank belongs with "Pulse of Memory," by Beth Dawkins. Much the same way that we here at the Scumm Institute preserve alternate histories through our exhibits and research, so too did this reality's inhabitants preserve memory through unique bioengineering. If anyone would like to participate in a little historical reenactment, just grab one of our rental swimsuits and jump right in! The Institute apologizes for any lingering bloodstains on our rental garb.

Moving through to our research wing, allow me introduce Sara Saab and the ongoing "Burrowing Machines" project. This work promises to provide the Institute with a new method for rapid soil excavation in alternate realities, just as soon as we figure out how to tamp down on the whole "hunger" thing a bit. Do be careful walking around these holes, people—it looks like we've had a few more pop up since my last tour.

Andrew Griffin's in-depth anthropological investigation, "Reptilian Barbarian and the Templum Solarium," offers us a fascinating look into a legendary warrior and their participation in an incredibly significant—and incredibly bloody—mythic adventure. We've heard that the "sword and board" reenactments we offer at the Institute are great for morale, even if our insurance provider disagrees. First aid's over by the bathrooms, by the way.

"Being Emily Was Too Hard," by Kieran O'Mant is a case study on experimental habitat design, with focus on the experience of long-term occupants facing an extended isolation. As you might have guessed from the stains on some of those pages, we here at the Scumm Institute prefer to start out by studying failed experiments before eventually moving onto the successful ones. But then, aren't the failures always more interesting? I think so.

"A Collection of Endings," by Leo Vladmirsky, is a similarly fatalist piece of field work, if not quite so bloody. Featuring first-hand accounts from a researcher who became deeply embedded within a maritime community on one alternate Earth, this project—ahem, sorry folks, this project always gets me a little teary-eyed, which is real troublesome for a single-celled organism who needs to hold on to their moisture. And, uh, also one who doesn't technically have eyes.

Finally, in our Scumm Institute "Kidz Korner"—which, to be honest, would be a lot safer for the little ones if we moved it to the beginning of the tour—we have the journalistic "Bureaucracy of Weird: UFO Myths Debunked!" by Paul C.K. Spears. Let the kiddos blow off some energy with our "G-Man Escape" obstacle course, or see if they can separate truth from government disinformation in our "Agency Alphabet Soup" ball pit.

Now, as we conclude our tour, I am... once again inexplicably alone, having lost my entire tour group through no fault of my own. Jeez, Scummy doesn't seem to mind, but I really feel like we could be doing something about guest retention on these tours. Maybe t-shirts, or something.

Oh well. There's always the next group.

PLANET SCUMM ISSUE #14

EXTINCTION EVENTS

SPARK & FIZZ BOOKS, 2022
Portland | Boston | Arcturus

BIOGRAPHIES

SPECIAL THANKS TO OUR FIRST READERS

We can't overemphasize the importance of our keen-eyed and open-minded team of volunteer first readers. Planet Scumm would be a shabby thing indeed if we were still sorting every submission in-house.

Special attention must be paid to the following folks for their devoted efforts in selecting stories for this issue, presented alphabetically.

- **A. KATHERINE BLACK** is scheduled to be a giant squid in her next life.
- **TARA LAMB** is a potato champion and forest witch.
- **SAM REBELEIN** doesn't write every day. Some days, it's just too nice out.
- **FRANK SMITH** is transforming into an owl.
- **DAN STINTZI** is pondering his orb.

AUTHOR BIOS

MAXINE SOPHIA WOLFF is a transgender writer from Virginia. Her work has appeared in *Scum Mag*, *Fusion Fragment*, and *Bleed Error*. She also writes interactive fiction.

MARIE VIBBERT has sold over 80 short stories to places like *Clarkesworld*, *F&SF*, and *Analog* and her work has been translated into several languages. Her debut novel, *Galactic Hellcats*, was on the British Sci-Fi Award long list for 2021. Her second novel, *The Gods Awoke*, comes out in 2022. By day she is a programmer in Cleveland, OH where she lives with her partner Brian and their wonderful kid Jen.

FRANK ORETO is a writer of weird fiction living in the wilds of Pittsburgh, PA. His stories have appeared in *Pseudodpod*, *Flame Tree Press*, and *The Magazine of Fantasy and Science Fiction*. When not writing, Frank spends his time creating elaborate meals for his wife and his ever hungering children.

DALE STROMBERG grew up not far from Sacramento, CA before moving to Tokyo, where he had a brief music career. Now he lives near Kuala Lumpur and makes ends meet as an editor and translator. His work has been published here and there.

LOGAN A. MARROW is a speculative fiction writer from Upstate NY, who has written for publications as wide-ranging as the horror magazine *Thuggish Itch* to political art collective *Do Not Research*. He frequently uses the pen names "Lucas A. Marlowe" and "Leonard MacAffee."

Recently, he has been featured as a finalist in *2000 AD*'s annual comic writing competition, and he is in the process of refining the manuscript for his first fix-up, a collection of short stories set in a beatnik burgerpunk dystopia. He can be found on most social media as @majordanby1.

BETH DAWKINS grew up on front porches, fighting imaginary monsters with sticks, and building castles from square bales of hay. Her fiction has appeared in *Analog* and *Apex Magazine*. She can be found on Twitter @BethDawkins and her website, BethDawkins.com.

SARA SAAB was born in Beirut, Lebanon. She now lives in North London, where she has perfected her 'resting London face'. Her current interests are croissants (and emojis thereof), amassing poetry collections, and coming up with a plausible reason to live on a sleeper train. Sara is a 2015 graduate of the Clarion Writers' Workshop. Her stories have most recently appeared in *The White Review*, *Clarkesworld*, and *The Dark*.

ANDREW GIFFIN teaches high school English in Richmond, Virginia, where he lives with his wife and two daughters. He is an autistic author whose previous writing can be found in *Cosmic Horror Monthly*, *The Dread Machine*, and *Abyss and Apex*.

KIERAN O'MANT is a UK-based author living in London. He has previously had poetry published in *Vagabonds: Anthology of the Mad Ones*.

LEO VLADIMIRSKY works in advertising and has created campaigns for clients as varied as IKEA, YouTube, The Kennedy Space Center, and XBOX. His fiction has appeared in *Fantasy and Science Fiction*, *Analog*, and several anthologies. He is working on his second novel. You can find his work at leovladimirsky.com.

PAUL C.K. SPEARS is a writer and lover of the weird and occult living in Cranston, RI. He has previously been published in *Weirdbook Magazine* and the *Enter the Rebirth Apocalypse Anthology*. He enjoys horror movies, tabletop roleplay games, and doing Wikipedia deep-dives about UFO encounters.

PLANET SCUMM CREW

EDITOR-IN-CHIEF

SEAN CLANCY's primary job is to *make word go right place* (but sometimes better). Ensign Clancy also acts as the current Herald of Scummy, blessed to transcribe every errant whim of our intergalactic space deejay, praying that the maniacal slime-bag achieves only half of his deranged fantasies.

This should be where Sean plugs a side project, but he's going to be shy and go for a meta joke that he'll later fail to justify to the rest of the team as "staying true to *Planet Scumm*'s irreverent roots."

MANAGING EDITOR

TYLER BERD is the herder of many cats for *Planet Scumm*. He acts as the ship's secretary, accountant, retail manager, and troubadour. Ty keeps his third eye trained on all the moving parts of the *Scumm*™ machinery. He prides himself for keeping the ship running only *slightly* behind schedule. Back on Earth, he is a teacher and musician.

Planet Scumm's benevolent(?) overlord, Scummy, grew to sentience from a poorly monitored boil behind Ty's ear. And the rest, as they say, is history.

CREATIVE DIRECTOR

ALYSSA ALARCÓN SANTO has learned to put her obsessive love of organization to use by laying out books, piloting the ever-growing art team, and making sure that the *Scummiverse*'s branding is cohesive. She occasionally has time for some artwork. Her time out-of-orbit is spent doing design work for NaNoWriMo, as well as freelancing on other comic, literary and/or disability-centric projects.

She infrequently remembers to post on instagram @alyssasantodesign or, even less frequently, on twitter at @traitorlegs.

PRODUCTION ARTIST

MAURA McGONAGLE, who also goes by 'Moe', is a bedraggled illustrator, comic artist, and a traveling resident of various artist alleys. Being a true professional, they have been rejected from most reputable—and disreputable—societies and were summarily marooned in space for their crimes. Rescued by Scummy, they are now ~~held captive~~ a happy disciple with no other interests, no sir.

They can be found hanging around on instagram at @mcmcgonagle or over on twitter at @doingartiguess.

PLANET SCUMM CREW

MARKETING DIRECTOR

SAM RHEAUME is a painter, illustrator, designer, writer, traveler, musician, printmaker, businessman, marketer, winelover, event planner, etc, etc. He is, and has been, an artist for a long time. The area in between media and methods has always been where he is most interested. Gray areas are where fear transforms into opportunity. His work can be found on various socials at @sirheaume.

INTRODUCING ANNA CATALANO, EDITOR AT LARGE

We got a sense of Anna Catalano's sci-fi sensibilities from her Issue #8 contribution "Lazarus." Since then she's been a thoughtful, powerhouse slush reader who has stepped up to join our strange and secret editorial meetings as a staff editor.

We thank her for her thoughtful, judicial, and aesthetic contributions in shaping the final slate of stories in this issue.

INTRODUCING LUCAS WISEMAN, CONTENT STRATEGIST

LUCAS X. WISEMAN is an enthusiastic maker of all things content, including but not limited to: advertising, blogs, and really good TikToks.

In his free time he writes novels, plays Dungeons and Dragons, doodles, drinks beer, builds LEGOs, and makes leather goods with his laser cutter. He can be found on instagram at @lucasxwiseman.

ANNA CATALANO is an Oregon-based author whose fiction has appeared in *Luna Station Quarterly*, *Planet Scumm*, and *Peculiar Journal*. She is also half of a co-writing duo signed to publish their debut contemporary romance novel under the joint pen name Sylvia Barry.

When she's not reading submissions and editing for *Luna Station* and *Planet Scumm*, Anna can be found binging Netflix, whittling down her enormous TBR pile, and trying not to kill any plants.

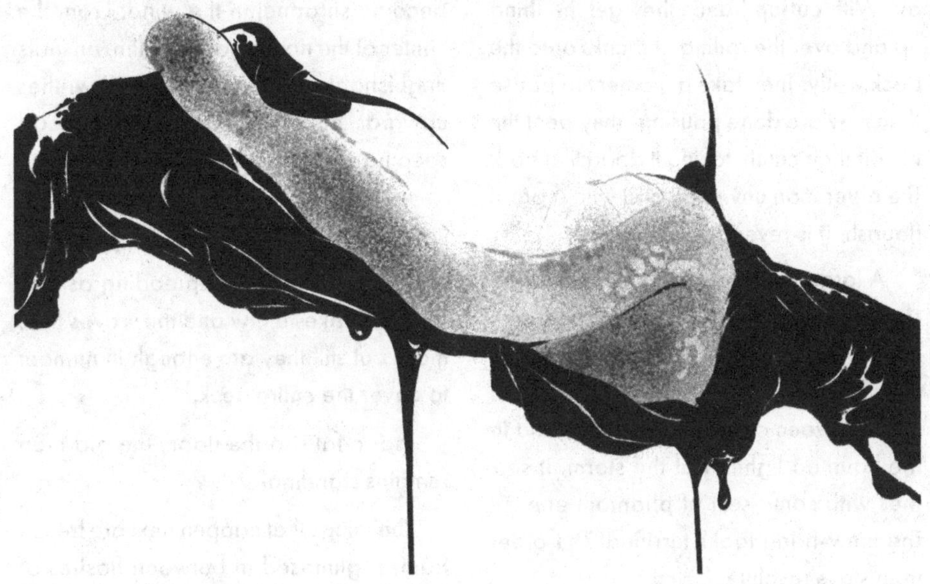

MAXINE SOPHIA WOLFF

COME THE BANSHEE

Off the weather-beaten shore of a city lit by green lights, a fishing boat thrashes in the coastal drop-off.

Surging beneath it, columns of water writhe with animated fury, stripping paint from the hull and pulling nails from the wood. A low sky swirls hungrily above the vessel, and there is a great deal of rain.

On the bow of this ship, there is a man we know but do not recognize. (Things come and go for us, knowledge not easily retained.) He's the spitting image of a fisherman: curly black hair, a beard streaked with gray, a strange sadness in his eyes. He stands pressed against the port-side railing, belly flush with the metal, hauling

something up from the water. The nets struggle with some great weight in the churning sea beneath him.

The toll is too great for his body, and he is losing ground. On his face, which is bent but gentle, sweat and saltwater mix into an indistinguishable frenzy. He's losing liquid too, not just line. It is a hot storm. He curses—spits and screams a little—but he does not stop hauling. A few moments pass before a crewman flies out from behind the covered helm and rushes to his elder's aid.

Together, they manage to fight back the spitting fury of the net, weathering the waves and the wind and the steam in the air. With cut-up hands they get the thing up and over the railing. It *thunks* onto the deck wetly. They take a moment to pause, then they are done pausing. They peel the net off their catch, taking it apart like bark. The older man unveils it, and with a great flourish, it is revealed.

A large wooden coffin, its wood long since made black by algae and the absence of light, lies on the deck. It drips with moisture and matter. Sludgy soil spills out from between cracks in the wood, and in the haunted lighting of the storm, it seethes with some sort of phantom energy. The crew-hand looks terrified. The older man stays resolute.

"What is it?!" The crewman asks over the rain.

"I don't know. A coffin."

Rain beats down around them.

"We'll have to go to the Priory."

The older man doesn't respond. He gnaws on his lower lip with his teeth.

"I'm going to open it."

"What? Why?"

"This is an omen, Isaac, I have to open it. There are rules." This silences the crewman—Isaac—whose face reddens, then drops to stare at the deck.

The older man moves forward, plucking a crowbar from a rain-battered rack. He takes it silently, brings its mouth to the coffin's wooden cover, and pulls upward. Nails screech as they are pulled from their long-submerged home and chips of wood

become shrapnel in the wind. From the center of the now-opened coffin, an indistinguishable blackness swells. It writhes upwards, bubbling up from the old wood, seeping over the sides of it.

They're *eels*, we realize, looking on. Hundreds of tiny black eels moving as one, seething as one, spreading as one. The wind takes a few and the waves take more but still they are enough in number to cover the entire deck.

Isaac falls to the floor. The old man remains standing.

The things that happen next are freeze frames, glimpsed in between flashes of lightning:

The coffin bursts into a glimmering fire.

A wave sweeps over the deck, reclaiming the eels.

The coffin is gone now, but the fire is still there.

The green light from the city flashes three times.

There is a burst of white—

When color returns, there is a horse's skeleton in the coffin's place, its bones picked clean and ashen. It too bursts into flames, painting the old boat in its light. The old man sees everything and then everything is gone, vanished into some unseen oblivion by the storm.

The two men exchange glances. They take a second to catch their breath. Then,

COME THE BANSHEE

with a silent determination, they go to the helm and head toward port.

✧

Maria sits inside the chest of her previous body. Her spine curves upwards and out from where it used to sit, the expended flesh all but split into unrecognizable pieces. Her legs are still stuck, which annoys her, so with a violent *snap* she wrenches her knees skyward, popping them loose. With a single movement, she pulls them out—out from the hollowed bones in which they grew, past paddings of fat and knotted, bitter muscles.

Maria likes to imagine herself as a crab when her body goes through this. It's somehow calming. So, she fills her head with crustaceans, and then she slips herself out and steps free. At her feet, her old body is a mess. The chest is shattered open, ribs broken and upright, torn flesh gaping like a basking shark in the shallows. She grimaces, and then sets to work with a broom.

She's still sticky with blood when she steps into the kitchen. She does her stretches right there in front of the fridge, naked and filthy. Once done, she plucks up an orange from the icebox and begins to peel and separate it. An ocean breeze flutters through the window behind her.

It is barely morning, still dark, and the air carries with it a strange smell—a seething something not dissimilar to pollen. At the base of the city, wreathed in sheets of busy wind, sits the harbor and its ghostly light. And on one of the docks... there is a crowd. Maria's eyes narrow and focus until the distance is made irrelevant. She sees the crowd clearly. It looks busy.

Maria is bored, and so she decides to go. Her schedule is clear anyways—the Priory hasn't given her work in a while. She wreathes herself in a black cloak, pops the hood over her feathered head, and leaves.

✧

"A horse?"

"A horse *skeleton*."

Isaac sits on a barrel, sand in his hair, looking a little delirious. Behind him, holy men from the Priory are busy blasting the fishing boat with a massive hose pulling sand from a nearby tank. Atop the tank, another holy man repeats a short blessing, ordaining the substance with cleansing power. A sharp cone of back spray mists the oval-shaped prayer masks of these priests with fine layers of sediment. One of them—a woman—is trying her best to clear the crowd.

"Can you tell me anything else?" Maria asks Isaac, her face hidden by a prayer mask swiped from the Priory's cart.

"I don't know. It was on fire. I saw green. I already spoke to the Prior about this, I don't know why I have to repeat it to you."

A coffin full of eels... A flaming horse skeleton...

Maria chews on these details, worry furrowing in her brow. "Is there anything else you can tell me?"

"No. Like I said, I already told the Prior all of this. If you want to know more, you should ask Brick. He saw more than I did—knows more about this stuff too. He's the one who opened it."

Maria grimaces. This was Brick's boat. His omen. Struck by realization, Maria's hidden face flushes red, and she excuses herself, cursing her own recklessness as she flees. If the Priory caught her speaking with Brick, she would have surely been punished. Such a thing is forbidden.

Her mind churns back to the omens. A coffin for death. Eels for secrecy. A horse for a bargain. This was Brick's omen, and *the Prior was here*. It starts to make sense with a sudden and terrible swiftness.

Maria moves like a wraith as she leaves, sticking to the shadows, nerves knotting in her stomach. When she gets home, she throws the stolen mask into the garbage and begins to prepare a frantic dinner. Three livers freshly delivered from the Priory, two oranges, and a glass of hot cider. She eats on her roof, basking in the dim green light of the city, wondering why the thread has finally decided to fray.

✦

We see Brick (we remember his name now and feel guilty for forgetting) sitting in a pew, his foot tapping nervously. He's trimmed his beard and freshened up. On his lap sits his prayer mask, unaffixed, with straps dangling past his knees. The mask is an old one, neatly carved from driftwood, yellow and green paint lathered on liberally. Two tusks curve out from the open mouth, ending in a point right where the wearer's ears would be. It is a dreadfully outdated heirloom. We wonder how long it has been since he's been to church.

Brick is not a small man, but in the Priory, he is made small. The old arc of the large, buttressed roof meets headily with the wooden walls around him, which are pockmarked with small and square windows of foggy stained glass. At the center of this main hall—surrounded by rows of circular pews—a small offering pit is dug into the ground. Along the walls there are cabinets full of masks, large amphoras brimming with sand, and tables swimming with candles. It is calm here, the air still and heavy with the scent of gravel.

After a moment, a man disturbs the silence. He comes from a door behind the pit, clad in heavy black robes and a gold prayer mask—similarly featureless to the masks at the pier. His steps land with an air of importance, as if the ground beneath his feet is soft and mossy, as if under that mask is nothing but teeth and smiling lips. He paces through the room and his pointed shoes clack loudly, silencing only as he takes a seat beside Brick.

"I figured you would come today," he says. "It's been too long."

Brick doesn't look up. His eyes are fixed on the floor.

"You know why I'm here," he says, in something halfway between a whisper and a growl.

The masked figure—the Prior—tilts his head. "I'm not sure I follow."

"Don't play games with me, Prior. A coffin full of eels? A flaming horse skeleton? I am no diviner, but I can read signs well enough. It's time we renegotiated our bargain."

"You seem to be misplacing memories, Brick. I recall no bargain between us."

Brick looks up. He has a seething anger brewing behind his eyes, and his lips curl into a grimace.

"You cannot run from omens, Prior. You of all people should know this."

The prior smiles, even though we cannot see it. Behind that mask, his lips are like a barnacle opening.

"I run from nothing."

"And yet still—"

"And yet, nothing. You come here to what, threaten me? Insult me? You come—unmasked—into my place of worship. Into my Priory. I will not have this. Leave, fisherman, and remember the debt that you owe me."

"Whatever debt I owe has long since been paid by her service. Don't think I don't know how you use her. Butchering for you. Your dirty work."

The Prior seethes, rises up, and suddenly he seems twenty feet tall. Black shadows writhe behind him.

"Out." He snarls, and it is less a command than an invocation. Brick raises his lips into a protesting snarl, but then obeys, dropping his mask to the floor.

"This is not over, Prior," he mutters as he leaves. "I will return."

By the time he hits the door, we have already scattered, and the Priory is silent once more.

✧

Maria lays down a circle of snakeskin, ties a small bell around her neck, and takes to her knees to pray. It's a silent prayer, lasting only a moment. She never really had much faith, but it's become something of a habit of late. Born out of guilt, maybe.

In the time since the Priory made her their weapon, Maria burned through over a hundred bodies. It wasn't the only side effect of their meddling. She doesn't seem to age at all—or if she does, it happens so slowly, it may as well be moot. They made her stronger, too. Of course, each time she sheds a body, part of her dies. And every time she dies, she makes a ghost.

Maria has made a lot of ghosts.

A splintered soul that always heals. A ghost for every shedding. She prays for them like this three days after each renewal, a ritual she fashioned after what little she remembers of her mother's religion. She wonders, not for the first time, what their lives must be like. Her half-formed specters, unable to pass on, tied to this bargain. She wonders if they have friendships. If they form communities. If they speak to one another.

Simultaneous to these thoughts, the analytical part of her brain is chewing on Brick's omen. *An early summer storm. A coffin full of eels. A phantom horse skeleton. A storm for changing winds?* She knows the signs and where they lead but is afraid to see their outcome.

And alongside both these concerns, beneath her skin and in the hollow bits of her bones, a new form is already growing, pushing old flesh aside, making room for fresh biology. It is painful already, but she does her best to ignore it. The sound of the rain helps. Across her many bodies, Maria has always loved the sound of rain.

She is knocked from her stupor by a knock at the door. *A knock?* Only the Priory knows she's here. That it might be Brick crosses her mind for a moment, but she discards the thought. They are not to see each other, he knows this. Who, then? She answers the door.

"Hello," says the woman in the doorway. She's tall, over six feet, a hulking creature clad in a leather duster and a strange hat that Maria does not recognize. Her face—both despite and because of its scarring—is oddly beautiful.

"Hi," Maria says, almost stupefied, forgetting how to speak, "Can I—can I help you?"

"Sorry about this."

The stranger grimaces, her lips pulled in a half frown. From a hidden place in her coat, she pulls a dagger, then jams it into Maria's chest. It slides through her skin and between her ribs like a javelin—perfectly placed. Maria staggers backwards and hits the ground.

"If it's any comfort to you," the woman says, lowering her head and stepping through the doorway, "I'm being paid well."

Maria crawls backwards on all fours like a spider, writhing in pain. Her vision triples and blurs with flashbacks. *Blood on her handkerchief. Brick's face—young still—laced with worry. The ride to the Priory where he wouldn't stop crying.*

"It's silver, if you're wondering. I'm sorry—I know it's not pleasant." The woman is inside now, and from behind her back she pulls out a folded crossbow.

Her strong arms undo the clasp and the device thunks together, wicked and grim. Maria is delirious, but somehow she staggers upright, black blood dripping from the knife lodged in her side. She kicks herself forward and rakes her long claws across the stranger's stomach. They find their mark but glance off something. *Armor.*

It takes only a moment for the stranger to redirect the momentum and take hold of Maria's wrists, forcing her to the ground. The stranger is pinning her down now and the crossbow clatters to the floor. With blinding speed, the stranger produces a second knife and drives it down toward Maria's heart. Maria wraps her clawed hands around the slick black handle of the blade and holds it at bay. But she's slipping. When the stranger readjusts her position and brings her boot down onto

Maria's neck, her vision starts to tunnel. But she lands a lucky knee strike to the stranger's stomach, and manages to wrestle the knife out of her hands.

Suddenly Maria is on top. She shrieks, making herself massive, and rains slashes downward but before they can connect, the stranger retrieves the first blade from Maria's chest and replants it violently three times. Maria howls, because she is good at howling. She spits up blood and scuttles on the floor like a spider, limbs disjointed and skittering.

With the desperate motion of a cornered animal, she flees through the sliding balcony door. The stranger takes a moment to rise, collecting her crossbow from the floor, then follows. But Maria, having taken up a perch on the roof, comes down onto the head of this woman like a terrible rain. She tears into her.

A crossbow bolt flies blindly into the horizon, nowhere close to its mark. Rivulets of blood gush from the assassin's neck, tendons flitting in the wind. She dies choking and breathless, her head nearly detached from her neck, her now useless arsenal of silver glinting in the low sun.

Beside her, Maria breathes hard and fast, still alive.

She hauls the heavy stranger's corpse back to her room. It's not an easy task, but Maria does it, mustering her faltering bits of strength. She drags it across the kitchen and, after much labor, props it against the mouth of her washing machine.

Still bleeding, she heads to her closet and searches through its mess. She pulls out a small black monitor. She pulls out many kinds of wires. She pulls out an old battery the size of a cinderblock, a keyboard, and a cable mounted with a long metal spike. When assembled, her contraption looks like an open circuit, wires connecting strange, incomplete devices.

Maria soon completes it. She strips the overcoat and armor from this tall, dead, stranger, and then slides the spike into her chest. As soon as the metal *shlunks* into place against bone, the small battery begins to glow a dusty green, and the monitor flickers to life. A program boots itself up with an electronic trill, then digital letters begin typing on the screen.

"*Ah... Fuck.*" It reads. "*You got me.*"

Maria sits down at her table, wincing at her many fresh wounds. On the keyboard, she types "Sorry."

"*It's alright. Risk of the job. How much time do I have in this thing?*"

"*Two minutes until your soul burns through the data disc. I don't have any spares.*"

"*Ha! Two minutes.*"

"*I need to ask who sent you.*"

"*Why would I tell you that?*"

"*Your allegiance is to coin. What good is coin now? Tell me.*"

"*You're bossy.*"

"*Maybe a little.*" Maria blushes a little bit. Flirting with a dead girl. She's bad.

"Hah! Fine. The Priory sent me. Told me there was a monster that needed killing. I didn't ask questions."

"The Priory? Are you sure?"

"Yes. I know who I do business with."

"Is this about the omen?"

"I don't know what you mean. I'm no expert in omens."

Maria pulls away from her keyboard, whispering breathlessly to herself. *A coffin... Eels...*

"Is there anything else you can tell me?"

"Yes. The Prior said something about a contract. I'm not sure what deal the two of you had, but whatever it is, it's been nullified. By his hands or by something greater, I'm not sure, but it won't matter."

By something greater. Maria furrows her brow.

"Okay. Thank you. I'm going to shut the machine off now."

"Okay. By the way, nice move, sneaking on top of me. I didn't see it coming."

Maria smiles a little. "Thanks. I'll be sure to bury you."

The dead woman doesn't say anything. Instead, the screen just flickers with static, waiting to be turned off. So Maria turns it off and there is the sound of power winding down. She then drags the body out to the yard, ties a small bell around its neck, and begins to dig a hole.

✧

We feel a tremor in the air. It's soft—barely noticeable above the whistle of the wind—but it rattles through the city like a heartbeat, or a sonar pulse, or an engine starting over. Overhead, the high noon sun is dimmed by low, gray, rolling clouds. Out toward the sea, waves come in gently, and boats rock in the shallows. The dock workers shuffle through the wood plank alleyways, hauling bags of oysters, bare backs calcified by sweat and salt. Over the sound of the city, we hear them sing:

With brine in her bosom and salt on her lips!

Come, The Banshee Come!

She'll sooner go drown ye then give ye a kiss!

Come, The Banshee Come!

Elsewhere, above the hill past the fish market, just before the construction lots where the first metal buildings are growing steadily, sits the Priory. It grimaces in the morning sun, soaking in color, its pale stone sweating moisture. Rings of sand encircle the structure, forming a sigil when looked at from above.

Three people are in the courtyard; Brick, the Prior, and a strange woman who looks like us. Behind them, the port is close and the white noise of water is distantly audible.

"This wasn't supposed to happen—" the woman says with a voice that sounds like ours. Hearing her voice makes us angry, bitter, even though we know none of this is her fault.

COME THE BANSHEE

At her feet, there is a small but growing puddle of blood being fed by three stab wounds in her chest. She stands injured, but poised, and continues speaking.

"—but we're here now."

The Prior grimaces behind his mask.

"Here to what, take vengeance?" he spits, spiteful.

"Maybe. Why did you send someone to kill me?"

Brick snaps his head toward the clergyman. "You did what?"

"It was defensive. Maria is *dangerous*, Brick. She's not your sister anymore—your sister died when we remade her. I'm sorry if we ever misled you."

The woman, Maria (*oh yes, that was our name*) snarls. She is seething in place, claws hanging at her waist, eyes hidden by her hood.

"Eels," she says. "A coffin. A flaming horse. You read the signs."

"Yes. A coffin for death. Eels for secrecy. A horse for bargains. Fire for entropy. *An old and secret bargain will soon end, badly.* I was merely protecting my interests."

Brick is looking at his sister. His old face furrows sadly.

"I only ever wanted to keep you safe, Maria," he says, calling over the wind. Everyone is distanced from each other, as if afraid to move—as if rooted in place. Brick's voice brims with sadness, and as he speaks, we begin to remember him

better. "The healers said you would die. The Prior offered me an alternative. I hope that you can forgive me."

Maria doesn't respond. Whether this is because she—because we—resent him, or simply because she—we—cannot find the words, we do not know. But the Prior breaks the silence.

"So, what happens now, then? A happy reunion? A bloodbath?"

"I was happy to be your assassin. I even enjoyed it." Maria snarls. "But you have betrayed your own intentions."

Now she turns toward Brick.

"You should've kicked that coffin back into the ocean, brother. But things are different now. Things have changed."

She takes a step forward, then with a sudden flash, she whips out the tall woman's folded crossbow. The mechanisms *thunk* into place, twin arms snapping forward. With a pop and a whistle, she pulls the trigger and the bolt spits through the air. It strikes the Prior's chest.

He yelps, staggering backwards, as blood sputters from his wound. His left knee hits the ground first, then his right, and then he falls forward. Brick looks on in either terror or adulation.

"You killed him..." he stammers, spit catching on his beard. "You killed the Prior..."

What Maria would have said here, we can only speculate. Maybe she would have killed Brick too. Maybe she would have held him, explained everything. But it doesn't matter, because before Maria can respond, the ground beneath them shakes and there is a shudder in the air—a fulfillment of terms that they played a part in but were not privy to.

Suddenly, the courtyard lurches and the sun starts to dim. Green strings of light crawl across the sky, like threads interweaving. The gulls caw louder. The wind whips quicker.

Something out at sea begins to stir.

"*Something greater....*" Maria says to herself, and we do not know what she means.

In the shallow bay of the port, the water is rising, displaced. Massive swathes of the unnatural flood rush through the fish market—splintering stalls into shrapnel, leveling carts. But the noise of fleeing people is wholly eclipsed by the sound coming from the water.

A terrible groan sinks into the wind, howling like a wraith. There is silence for a moment, then a loud pop, and something starts to rise.

It comes up from the shallows, its skin marred by crimson channels that crackle with red lightning. Its seaweed hair hangs down over its eyes, almost to its breasts, which are red and swollen. The air fills with the terrible stench of fish skin, and with a lurching step, the titanic creature brings its barnacled foot down through the roof of a container ship, crushing it into the seafloor. It howls and the sound rips through the air like flesh burning away.

To himself, like a child cooing, Brick continues the song of the sailors.

Shipwrecks could snuggle in the curve of her hips,

Come, the banshee come!

The grace and the terror of the swimming abyss,

Come, the banshee come!

Maria doesn't hear this, because Maria is already gone. With a key she swipes from the Prior's body, she raids his treasury—payment for the bargain that was broken. When she leaves, she does not look back at the destruction. Instead she keeps her eyes fixed ahead of her, like a predator. Like a thing that survives.

She is not looking when the colossus opens its mouth and breathes fire into city streets.

She does not see her city die.

We follow her, our ghostly forms bleating in the daylight, and pour ourselves down her throat. In her stomach—in this place from which we came—new flesh sets itself into place against old flesh, and we file in beside it. We are remade and rebound—a small justice in a sea of things far beyond our station.

MARIE VIBBERT

SINGLE MALT SPACECRAFT

ORIGINALLY PUBLISHED IN LIGHTSPEED MAGAZINE, JUNE 2020

The first time Fresia tasted scotch, it was true love. She was twenty-two. Her boyfriend had just turned twenty-one and had gotten a bottle of Glenlivet from his dad. He poured a shot for himself and for his friend, but none for Fresia.

"Come on," she said, "I want to taste it."

"Girls don't like whisky," he said. "Trust me, you'll hate it."

"Let me find out for myself."

"Not for what this costs, sorry."

The friend gasped over his empty shot glass. "Oh, that's good."

Her boyfriend put the whisky on the top of the fridge, where he knew Fresia was too short to reach. Later, when the guys were in the next room, she climbed on the counter to get it down and drank straight from the bottle. It tasted like lying in the sun on a perfect summer day, like only the best parts of caramel. She took another, larger swig, and didn't wipe the lip before putting it away.

✧

Fresia's ship broke through the cloud layer and approached Burke Lakefront Spaceport over the slate-colored waves of Lake Erie. The buildings were the same faux-1950s revival she remembered, but they were dingier, glass gone to smeary opacity, the lawns unkempt. A lot changed in forty years, though to her it had been two weeks.

Fresia hoped looks weren't everything. She banked to land and the bottle next to her foot tipped against her. Single malt scotch: Glen Fresia, forty years aged. A very small batch, a very special batch.

Fresia opened the cargo doors and got a face full of muddy lake scent. This was her third trip home, her third gamble, throwing herself forty years ahead of Earth so she could keep her dream alive. Her Glen Fresia. Last time there'd been a pair of softly glowing silicone loader bots. This time she faced a crowd of human laborers. Surly human laborers.

A young man detached himself from the crowd. "Well come, Miss Fresia."

He said 'welcome' like two words and 'Miss' like he was translating it. How much had language drifted this time?

"Are you the port relativity liaison?"

He bowed.

"Nope. I'm Stuart. You would remember my grandmother." He held out the metal card she'd given to her home business agent, who had refused paper on what felt like religious grounds.

She took the card, afraid that it was the only surviving artifact of her last visit. "What happened to this place?"

"The war," Stuart shrugged. "But Miss should make a killing. Nostalgia is large these days. And dang..." he picked a ceramic superhero up out of its foam cradle. "I haven't seen one of these since I was a child."

"Is my storage locker intact?" The warehouses near at hand looked like rotted teeth.

"Nope. Grand salvaged the contents. Moved all south during the war, and back again. Little different location. I show you." He set the superhero reverently in its place and waved to the porters. "Care this!"

The new warehouse looked like a sand-castle version of a barn. Stuart caught her staring. "Slurock. You have this when you were home last?"

"No. What is it?"

"Silicone mud mix sprays out of a hose. Goes up fast. Flexible for earthquakes. Ugly as butt, right?"

"I wouldn't pick it." Fresia wished he'd move faster.

Stuart passed his wrist over a sensor on a post to open the door. So they were doing it that way now. One hundred and twenty years had passed here since her first trip out, but there were always doors, always some means of opening them. The interior walls looked like marbled plastic and were probably another new material she'd never heard of. The doors just looked like doors, though.

Fresia felt her shoulders unclench the minute she saw her casks. *Here* was something timeless. She stroked the wood she'd abandoned to the vagaries of decades a few weeks ago. Next to it were the business ledgers, hard copy to ensure they survived, and what had been a top-of-the-line data interface forty years ago. Fresia flipped the little box open and the screen projected above it.

"Is this going to work for my sales and purchases?"

"Not sure. The...datainfrastructures suffered." He pronounced 'data infrastructures' like a single, multisyllabic word learned phonetically. "Grand saw it coming, though. Tracked your holdings and banks and transferred as need."

"Bucking for a tip?"

"You pay my family well," he said, with the careful nonchalance of someone bucking for a tip.

Stuart showed her how to approve purchases on the device embedded in his wrist. They were using ceramic casks now, lined in printed oak. She worried over the effect on flavor, but Stuart insisted there was no supplier for real oak casks. She transferred a bonus to Stuart and made a gift in his grandmother's memory to a charity.

"Looks like I won't be upgrading the ship," she said. Not terrible. This was not the worst she could have found things. Glen Fresia would live another day. "Tell me, what's new and cheap and made of something that ages badly?"

He looked disappointed.

"How you get into this..." he waved his hands helplessly.

"Junk dealing?"

He narrowed his gaze like sunlight in a lens, like he was trying to burn understanding into her. "I mean... your ship? This independence?"

"How'd I get out of my trucking contract?

His response was a widening of the eyes, eagerness. His grand had to have told him the story: Intrepid trucker makes it good on a lucky stash of comic books.

"You're trying to get me to brag so I like you."

Stuart ducked his head but couldn't hide his smile. "It working?

Fresia spent the night with Stuart. He wasn't handsome, but he was enthusiastic, and she felt a need to press flesh to flesh.

The guilt set in before her sweat cooled. Liking Stuart was a betrayal of her idea of herself as a celibate space pirate, sworn off men, giving her heart to the more reliable affections of scotch whisky. And she knew she'd never see him again.

God, she was selfish. Did she really think it would always be worth it?

Too uncomfortable to sleep, she explored Stuart's apartment. It felt familiar. Possibly it was old-fashioned, an artifact of the family's business selling nostalgic items from exactly forty years ago. Stuart followed her into a kitchen that looked like his grandmother's. He put his hands on her bare hips and kissed her shoulder.

"Hungry?"

She wasn't particularly, but it was a chance for fresh food. "Yeah."

Stuart fried eggs wearing silk sleep shorts. Downy hairs on his stomach, skin taut and smooth as eggshell. It was the best he'd looked.

"When will you...quit?" he asked. He looked back when she didn't answer. "I... meaning it must be lonely, all those years."

Now he was bucking for more than a tip. "Feels like a few weeks to me."

He slid a plate in front of her. It smelled of garlic and cheese, comforting and savory. "A few weeks can be lonely, too."

The eggs were a little too hot, crispy on the edges—exactly how she liked them.

"I have Whisky," she said, meaning her cat, but she could tell from the sudden widening of his eyes that he worried she was an alcoholic.

Well, she loved scotch, too.

She finished the eggs, felt tender toward Stuart for worrying, and they made love again, long and slow and this time she fell asleep after, and that was good.

In the morning, Stuart wouldn't look at her as they signed the final agreements.

That wasn't to be helped. It stung leaving people behind when she first signed up, and it would sting again. She imagined the hard acceleration pushing the emotion right out of her.

It didn't.

When the gees leveled off, she curled up in her beanbag chair in the rec room. The week of travel stretched before her, empty. Weeks could be lonely, too.

Whisky sauntered in, yowling his displeasure at the AutoCat Pet Crate decanting him. He never got the hang of acceleration-gravity and would mew piteously and slink on the floor, showing his horror at being heavier than expected. The Auto-Cat kept him safe from that, but it was akin to a day-long trip to the vet.

She crawled to him. "I'm sorry, baby. Take off and landing are awful."

He avoided her with his chin raised in righteous indignation. Well, he'd come around when she started a movie.

As always, her agent—she had to stop calling him Stuart in her head—had provided her with a curated collection of film and books from the past four decades. It was in the original contract, for her own good. She had to try. Try to catch up, understand, relate. The memes slipped from under her so fast. She had to be ready to integrate with society when she hit the ground for the last time.

The first movie she queued up didn't make sense at all: footage of streams and fields, uncut flying paths that crawled under leaves or swung up to where a person's head should be.

SINGLE MALT SPACECRAFT

Whisky yowled and hopped neatly into her lap, turning once and dropping into a puddle of warm orange fur. She was forgiven. *Take that, Stuart.* She had Whisky, and whisky, to keep her company.

She uncorked the latest scotch. It had a wheat-like touch to its mellow oak. Not as caramel as the last batch. A delightful change.

She'd had good luck, overall. Her first batch started with the purchase of a five-year old cask and it had come out fragile forty years later, vanishing on the tongue with sharpness and clarity like an icicle. She switched to buying new mash and barrels. One cask in the second batch failed—a slight air leak that might not have damaged it in ten years had turned the contents weak in forty. Maybe the new-fangled barrels would be a good thing. Safer. There could be new flavor influences to discover.

She scratched behind Whisky's ears. The next film started, and it made even less sense. Discordant music fading in and out, flashes of still images. How depressing and futile her little film festival was! A condensed trip to a past skipped over.

She left the player going in the background and re-read 'A Wizard of Earthsea' while Whisky purred on her stomach.

In the middle of the second chapter, she fell out of the story, thinking about Stuart, about his blue silk shorts and the way he leaned back on the kitchen counter, half-turned to her. He was living in fast-forward.

How many fried eggs had he eaten? The thought hurt. She pushed it down. Any guy could feel perfect if you only knew him for a day.

A week later, the ship decelerated.

Style and culture changes were slower on Glieseg. The spaceport building added two new wings, and moving sidewalks had been put in. She couldn't quantify it, but it felt like there were more people—maybe that was just the sidewalks moving them faster.

She found, to her horror, a thriving nostalgic trinkets market along the arrivals bay. Truckers like her setting Earth imports out under cloth awnings. The second table had the wax butterflies Stuart had suggested she buy. Swarms of them. Well, no money in those, then.

Her previous agent, Tracy, met her, still recognizable for his lopsided smile, leaning on the arm of his middle-aged daughter.

"We're anxious to see the news from Earth!" he said.

"Still not accepting bank notes?"

He laughed. "We'll upgrade and repair your vessel and feed and house you, never fear. It's a public good, that you bring novelties and stories."

Fresia gestured at the bustling market of other truckers. "Seriously? What am I adding?"

Tracy patted her arm. "Oh, how you capitalists think! A thing doesn't have to be unique to be welcome. Now be happy!

See what I've arranged—goods from the new colonies for you to take back to the mother planet."

"New colonies! I miss a lot when I'm en route. Still no faster than light radio?"

"How would that even work?" the daughter scowled.

Tracy cackled delightedly and they spoke rapidly in a patois. Daughter rolling her eyes and gesturing, father waving ideas away with one hand. They were close speakers, people who touched a lot. Fresia felt the empty air between her and them.

She sleepwalked through the day, feeling like she'd left a kettle on back on Earth.

In the morning Fresia was loaded up with news and data files, as well as the promised exotic trade goods—a crate of biological specimens suspended in sparkling energy fields.

"I was lucky to see you twice," Tracy said, smiling-sad in the way only old people could pull off. He shook her hand a long time. "My grandchild, Patra, will greet you next time. I am training her. Unless you wish to stay?" His fingers closed, tugged on hers.

Fresia couldn't bring herself to speak in response. She hugged him. She knew when she first set out that she'd end up not at home on either side of her route, but she hadn't *really* known. What was the difference between intellectual-knowing and experienced-knowing?

Tracey probably knew.

The colonist's film collection started with a news report specially made for her to bring to Earth. Usually she liked these prosaic, easily digested stories. This time, it felt like a highlight reel from four seasons of a sport she didn't follow. Names, dates, numbers... did any of it mean anything?

She had a double shot, neat, of Glen Fresia Number One. Life wasn't so bad. She lived in endless luxury of fine alcohol.

She tried to gather Whisky into her arms, but he turned and hissed at her. She gave him extra food and a wax butterfly to destroy. She thought about the casual intimacy between Tracy and his daughter, between him and this granddaughter she would meet next time.

Stuart could be a grandfather by the time she got back to Earth. She started to look forward to meeting his kids, seeing what sort of people they turned out to be, wondering what they would reveal about him in their attitudes and manners.

Just outside of Earth-controlled space, Fresia was seized with certainty that no one was living on the home planet anymore. Where was the air traffic control signal?

A long, anxious second past the usual time, the signal was there.

Burke Lakefront had a strange, organic feel this time, like the buildings had melted or grown fungus on them. The lake had retreated, a beach of dark sand separating the old break wall from sluggish waves.

She was met by a dour-faced, boney man who introduced himself as Cic.

"Are you Stuart's son?"

Cic spoke stilted, formal English, and almost sneered as he identified himself as Stuart's cousin, once removed.

"Stuart died unexpectedly. Heart attack at 43. He did not make adequate arrangements for your business." Cic's lip curled in distaste as he handed her a slender package. "He left you these."

It was a packet of letters, a one-sided conversation of years. Fresia cried, not because Stuart was particularly special to her, but because he wasn't.

Cic studied the port lights over her head like a surly teen avoiding watching his parents kiss.

"Sorry," she cleared her throat, straightened her spine. "Let's go." It would all be worth it, for the whisky. Wasn't that her agreement with herself?

The warehouse was still there but had grown soft folds, like a cake left out too long. The casks were not. The data link Stuart had left for her didn't work.

Cic said, "It would not matter if it did. The bank is gone. You have no dollars."

Still reeling from the news about Stuart, woth half her mind on what his letters might contain, Fresia wasn't sure she'd heard correctly.

"No dollars? My money? Nothing is left? Where is my whisky?"

"I took it as payment." He looked like he thought this a generous concession.

"Payment for what?"

"For my services in your absence."

"I need you to tell me what happened to my whisky. I need my ship serviced so I can take off again. I need to buy more whisky."

Cic folded his arms. "How is this my problem?"

✧

After several hours of negotiation and grudging translation, Cic admitted he'd moved the casks to the bottling facility, but hadn't been able to pay for processing. Fresia arranged to have the whisky bottled in exchange for a percentage of the yield, with the box of bio specimens and the tchotchkes from forty years ago going to Cic to pay for whatever it was he felt he'd done for her.

He certainly hadn't safeguarded her business. No new casks of fresh liquor to age. There would be no tryst on this trip! She spent the night back on her ship, eating the last of her supplies from the colony.

"Damn you for dying, Stuart." She set a shot in front of the empty chair opposite her.

Compared to Stuart, losing her amassed fortune impacted her emotionally like losing a particularly long game of solitaire. They had only been numbers in a computer. It wouldn't bother her at all if she could get back on her route!

She had always known she had a limited number of trips in her tank. Despite that, she hadn't formed a Plan B.

The security system projected an image of Cic in front of her. He was knocking on the cargo door. Ugh. He looked even more of a prick in side-view.

She opened a channel rather than get up from her sulk. "What do you want?"

"You have no fuel. There is no reason to hold on to this ship. You will sell it to me."

Fresia slammed down her bowl. Not that he heard that. He was squinting up at the security light over the hatch. Whisky hopped on the table and started eating the spilled oatmeal. She pushed him off. "That's bad for you, cat." He ignored her.

Fresia grabbed a bottle of Glen Fresia Batch Two (it came in particularly heavy glass) and stomped to the cargo door. She brandished the bottle. "I'm not selling. Not to you."

Cic was nonplused. "The port will demand rent."

"You could get me in the sky again, you cheat."

His cold expression didn't change. "I could. For your whisky."

Fresia lowered her hand. She looked down at the lovely, caramel-colored liquid sloshing in the clear bottle. She had a store on the ship, one case from each batch. "How much?"

"All of it."

"Oh, fuck OFF." She slammed the door shut. Back in the galley she watched him shrug and walk away on projection.

Glen Fresia Batch Four came out peaty, complex and dark despite the mellowing of age. No discernable new flavor from the artificial oak. It paired well with instant oatmeal and depression.

The next day, probably at Cic's invitation, the port authority visited. The chief officer had bushy ginger hair and a little tablet she consulted after every sentence, as though it was transcribing or translating for her.

"We do not accept barter," she said, after Fresia offered a bottle of whisky.

"It's very valuable!"

A glance down, a word mouthed, a glance up. "It is not currency."

"For the love of Jupiter—no, don't translate that," Fresia was already frustrated with how slow the conversation was going. Of course, now the officer was checking her plea not to check. "Don't you know anyone who would be willing to trade scotch for cash?"

The officer's eyes widened. She didn't check her tablet. "Scotch?" she asked, with perfect, clear understanding.

A lucky break at last! Fresia waggled the bottle. "I don't suppose you'd mind a sip while we haggle?"

 SINGLE MALT SPACECRAFT

The officer looked adorably heartbroken. "We must... propriety... no bribes."

Cic skulked just outside the cordon for Fresia's ship, looking like a cat watching a fish gasp its last.

Fresia put down her bottle. "No bribes. But if you put me in touch with someone who can buy my scotch," she paused to let her reading catch up. "I will then have money from that sale for fees."

"We do not have authority. We cannot contact food merchants." But this woman did care. Fresia could see that. She cared about scotch.

Fresia put her arm around the official's shoulders. "How would you like to help humanity itself?"

"No bribes."

Fresia nodded. "No bribes. A legitimate business deal, and a public good. If you can't put me in touch with a food merchant, can you put me in touch with a government?"

The official looked doubtful, but she also kept looking at Fresia's bottle.

"That would not... be against the rules."

Fresia left Earth for the last time, misty-eyed and much poorer—she'd ended up trading all but one bottle each of her hard-gotten whiskies. (The open bottles, which she had to keep.) She had her fuel and bills paid enough that the creditors wouldn't stop her from launching.

No Glen Fresia Batch Five aging, alas, but she had something better in her hold: Four bio-stasis beds full of tiny, freshly-sprouted barley plants. Twenty packets of dried yeast. Peat moss and oak saplings. All through an agreement with the Scottish Cultural Union.

They were happy to have her promise to stop selling American-aged scotch on Earth. She'd find someplace in the stars to plant her fields, some place she could settle down and watch them grow, official property of Scotland—minus reasonable personal use.

Glen Stuart had a nice, Scottish ring to it. The future tasted malty, with hints of hope.

FRANK ORETO

ALL OUR MISSING PIECES

Gail stepped from the damp streets into the warm interior of City Grinders. She walked here three days a week to pick up her workmates' coffee orders. Her group leader thought the walk showed she was a team player. Her Personal Care Algorithm even sent her a healthy initiatives badge.

Gail would have come every day—and not for the calories her PCA said she burned. She came for Ruben. He smiled at her from behind the counter. Gail's stomach turned somersaults, even after all this time.

She walked toward him and almost sprawled over a man on all-fours wearing the green coveralls of the custodial track. The man grunted and pulled himself up. Thinning gray hair betrayed his age.

Poor guy, Gail thought. *He's probably nearing mandatory work-stop. Maybe, after a life in custodial, he's even looking forward to it.* But Gail could not imagine living out her last years in a robot-assist cube village.

The man gave Gail a small bow. "My apologies, Manager," he said. "I was looking for something." On a low table nearby sat a jigsaw puzzle, complete but for one piece.

"My fault—I should watch where I'm going." Gail felt something underneath her shoe. Bending, she plucked a puzzle piece from the floor. "I think I found what you're looking for."

The man took the piece from her hand.

"Thank you," he said to her in a dazed voice. "I don't want to sound rude, but could you please not touch the puzzle while I'm gone?"

"Sure," said Gail.

The old man nodded his thanks and practically ran out of the shop.

"You made old Charlie's day," Ruben said. He'd come from behind the counter and stood close enough to risk a fraternization warning. Gail could feel the heat of his breath.

"Why didn't he just finish it?" she asked.

"Damned if I know. He's worked on that puzzle for almost a year. Must be pretty hard."

"Maybe he's just terrible at puzzles."

"Maybe so. I offer to help, but he never lets me. Always says 'It must be by my hand alone. There are rules, Ruben.'"

Gail stood next to the man she loved. Instead of falling into his arms, she looked at the puzzle.

It didn't seem an odd way to spend those precious moments. For them to be together the way Gail wanted was forbidden, and they'd already shared the stories of their lives over hundreds of five-minute conversations. She knew about Ruben's three sisters. Two in the medic track, one lost on a subversion charge. She knew he was happy with his track in culinary retail. Or would be, if not for the cross-track anti-fraternization laws. Ruben knew about the solid, companionable husband Gail went home to at work-cease. The husband she had never loved despite a ninety-two percent algorithmic match.

They both knew their world balanced on an ecological and social knife-edge.

As a Manager, Gail understood more than most that the algorithms guiding their lives really worked. Maybe the algorithms didn't bring true love, but they did ensure the human race's survival. Wasn't that more important than the desires of two people? And if you answered no, well, that's why there was an enforcement track.

The puzzle showed a sun-dappled lakeshore giving way to a forest. A cottage stood in the distance, smoke drifting from its chimney. Real forests had disappeared before Gail was born. She wondered how it would feel, surrounded by trees.

A siren wailed. Reflexively, Ruben and Gail stepped away from each other. Her shin brushed the coffee table and a corner puzzle piece fell.

Gail threw herself to the floor. Desperately, she felt beneath the low table. *It's just a puzzle piece*, she told herself. But somehow, she knew she'd done something unforgivable.

The sirens grew louder.

Charlie burst back in. A tall, dark-skinned woman with gray hair held his hand.

She wore the ash-colored uniform of the enforcement track.

Charlie glared down at Gail. "What did you do?"

For a moment, Gail thought he might kick her.

"Wait, I found it," said Ruben. He leaned over to put the puzzle piece back in its spot.

"No, the rules!" Charlie shouted.

Ruben checked himself, and the piece fell to the table.

Charlie snatched it up. He pressed the piece back into the corner where it had come from, but it wouldn't fit. Gail could swear the tiny cardboard shape warped and stretched as the old man tried to work it in.

Outside, the shriek of brakes replaced the sirens.

Charlie tried putting the corner piece in the empty slot near the center instead. It slid in seamlessly. Then he took the last piece from his pocket and finished the puzzle. Charlie turned to the woman he had entered with.

"Do you trust me, Elizabeth?"

Elizabeth looked at Charlie, then down at the puzzle.

"I do, you old fool," she said, and they stepped up onto the table. Charlie smiled down at Gail and Ruben.

"The puzzle is yours now. Find your place."

"Nothing's happening," said Elizabeth.

Charlie pulled the woman close. "There are rules, Elizabeth."

He laughed, then kissed her. As their lips met, Charlie and Elizabeth slipped into the puzzle as if they had stepped into deep water.

A moment later, four hard-faced men in ash-gray suits pushed inside the shop. A wide man with an air of authority questioned Ruben with his eyes.

Ruben pointed. "There's a delivery door in the back."

Two enforcement officers went that way.

As Gail rose, she pushed hard on the coffee table. Puzzle pieces rained down onto the floor, changing as they fell. Gail caught glimpses of sand and waves, a seagull's wing. She had always wanted to see the ocean, but the water wasn't safe these days, and seagulls had gone extinct when Gail was in kinder-track.

"Clumsy me," said Gail. She collected a few pieces, laying them on the table.

An enforcer, round-faced and earnest, picked up a piece, eyeing the others. Gail took it gently from his hand.

"Let me. I made the mess." He gave her a nodding bow and stepped away.

Besides, Gail thought, as she fit two pieces together, *there are rules.*

   ALL OUR MISSING PIECES

DALE STROMBERG

PHARINEXIN

It happens at Glenvale Mall. Nurul is at the rock store, looking at geodes. Somebody shouts. A series of pops. For a moment, nothing makes sense. Then she realizes. Active shooter.

There's no time to do anything before she's hit. Without knowing how or why, she finds herself face-down on the beige floor tiles. A bullet in the back. Like a red-hot spike hammered into her. And fear. The awful conviction: *I will not live past this moment.*

Yelling. Confusion. A woman shrieking, no, no, no.

Someone kneels next to Nurul. Tells her to keep still. A security guard. Pulling something from his belt. The unmistakable green and black spray can. Of course. They're all equipped with it now.

Tell him to stop, she thinks desperately.

◆

Nurul's father was a Mender. He had a power that only one human in ten million is born with: to heal within minutes from any nonlethal wound. Menders did well to keep a low profile, but somehow TKS Heavy Industries found him.

He wasn't the only one TKS kidnapped. There were urban legends, though years passed before *60 Minutes* broke the story that led to investigations and indictments.

By then, it was too late for him.

Here is what Nurul learned from the televised hearings: At a secure research facility outside of Palm Beach, her father was used as a subject for weapons testing. They began with daggers and bayonets made of experimental carbon steel to be marketed to the military. Seven days a week, between 8 a.m. and 8 p.m. with a twenty-minute break for lunch, he was strapped to a gurney and sliced open, again and again, over every part of his body. Results were carefully videoed and cataloged.

They did this with all of them. Cut the same Mender the same way ten times, a hundred, a thousand. Watch the wound heal. Do it again, differently, controlling for other variables. Reams of data, invaluable to R&D.

After that came firearms, fragmentation grenades, flamethrowers, corrosive chemical agents. TKS developed ingenious means for keeping their test subject an inch from death: PBA (partial body armor), nurses trained in MLM (minimal lifesaving measures), and so on. How far from a grenade blast must the subject be to not to lose a limb? How many toes, on average, can be shot off with a pistol before the subject blacks out? In what proportion do the frequency and amplitude of deafening noise each contribute to the bursting of eardrums?

Nurul never brought herself to watch the video of his final, fatal munitions trial—

the video that convicted half a dozen TKS executives and two lead researchers. It's on YouTube, if she wants it.

Her father was deep-voiced, slow to anger, patient in explaining how things worked or why she had to follow the house rules. He had a shy smile, sad brown eyes, pianist's fingers. Nurul had told herself for years that he must be dead, but, once it was confirmed, and once she knew how it had happened, heartbreak and horror washed over her. The executives' prison sentences were cold comfort—most were out again in under two years.

The worst part was Pharinexin.

The wonder drug.

TKS wasted no opportunity for profitability. Her father's Mender physiology was a goldmine for pharmaceutical development. And there was no shortage of tissue samples for researchers to analyze; the janitors were bagging the stuff up daily. The result: Pharinexin. The power of the Menders, available over the counter. This mysterious gift, which it happens Nurul never inherited, was bestowed now on every paying customer. The jailing of a few executives was not going to keep something this valuable off the market for long.

So. It happens at Glenvale Mall.

She's at the rock store, looking at geodes. Somebody shouts. A series of pops. She's hit. Face-down on the beige floor tiles. A bullet in the back.

I will not live past this moment.

The security guard kneels beside her. "Keep still." Pulls the unmistakable green and black spray can from his belt. They're all equipped with it now.

Tell him to stop, she thinks desperately.

No—tell him to hurry up.

No.

Her father suffered and died to create that abhorrent spray can. No.

If anyone deserves to benefit from what befell her family, it *is* her family. Yes.

To use Pharinexin is to cooperate with her father's killers in her own treatment. No.

Strangers will use it. Why shouldn't she?

Because they killed him.

He would say, use it.

But yes is wrong. And no is wrong.

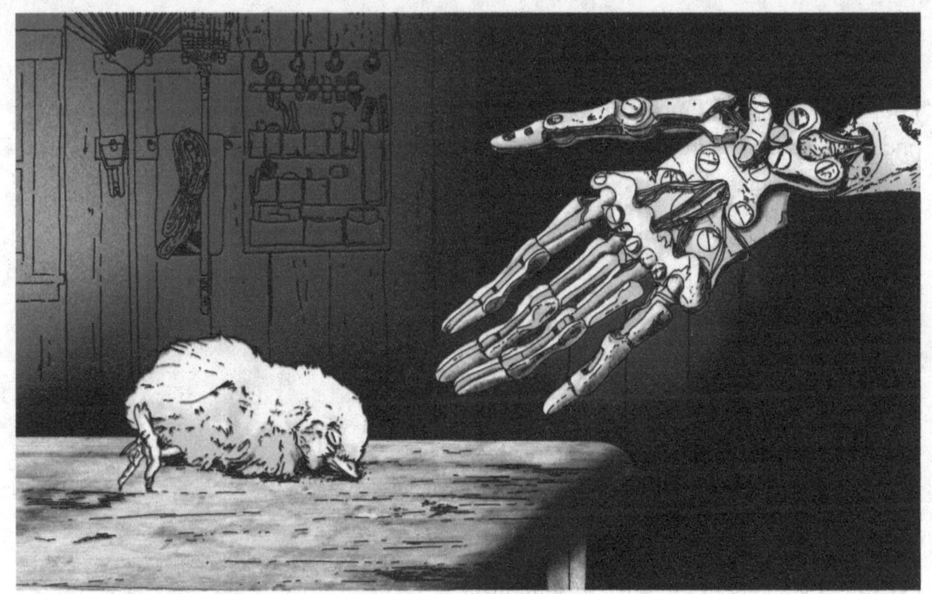

LOGAN A. MARROW

THE GARDENER

Robbie tended the garden. It was a great wide one, high up on an isolated hill deep in Maine. Robbie had seen no humans for quite some time now.

He sat patiently, recharging each morning, waiting for his solar power banks to reach at least 70% before turning loose on the twenty foot by twenty foot patch of dark soil.

Robbie had no fertilizer, something he was programmed to ask for once every four weeks if he were growing nutrient-dense vegetation like he was now, *101100*. The crops suffered for it a little, but not much. Robbie was not programmed to make his own fertilizer either, he didn't have the means. He was an old model, one of the last of his kind ever made. He still performed his job dutifully, with or without the man or woman there to watch. He didn't know it, but he was falling apart.

A flitting three-note melody played from a speaker on top of Robbie's head, *101010*. It was time to get up.

He stood up slowly and began towards the tool shed, his foot catching on a rock a little. He might have been able to detect it at one time, but his front motion sensor was corroded, needed replacing. Robbie paid no mind to this. Wires were crossing that should not be crossed, sending nonsensical messages that should not be sent. Every day now he was losing more and more of his finer functions, and it was impossible to tell how long he would have before becoming completely kaput.

He did not worry about falling apart, he had no diagnostic programs to run. It was not within his capacity to worry.

Robbie opened the tool shed. There was an iron hoe hanging by its head from two wooden pegs nailed into the wall. He picked it up. It was rusty from lack of care. The handle was beginning to rot, it was a well loved instrument. Robbie gripped it with both hands and made his way to the garden.

The garden lay surrounded by forest and acres of open fields, the man and woman's old farmhouse just a few dozen yards distant. In three rows, Robbie planted what he could with the seeds he could find from scouring the inside of the man's garage. Many of them were old, couldn't germinate, but a surprising and eclectic assortment of them took root and provided a good variety of plants to tend. Checkered different colors and producing a mess of fragrances, on any given row of Robbie's garden there were pumpkins, sunflowers, tomatoes, watermelons, peppers, mountain laurels, radishes, rhubarb, black-eyed-susans, peonies, potatoes, orchids and pea pods.

Today, Robbie would begin hoeing the rest of the patch that had not yet been divided. He walked over to the empty side of the garden, struck his hoe into the ground, and began methodically dragging up little clumps of dirt in a neat line toward the other end of the patch.

Inside him, circuits fired. Connecting and cutting off again, a message that he had dragged up enough of a clump, *000101*, a message that he had reached grass, finished the row, *010110*, a message that he should begin a new row spaced eight inches to the right, *000111*.

Robbie worked like this for half an hour, making neat lines in the dry, dark earth. He was this amalgamation of messages, of purposes, no other life than this. He plowed on, up and down, from left to right.

✧

Robbie stopped for a second, and looked at the wriggling thing. It was ugly, but he didn't know it, being only made to understand aesthetic beauty—symmetry and color saturation and fullness, as it related to vegetation. This thing was smaller, something pathetic, though he couldn't understand that either.

It sat in a pile of twigs, flapping around. Something circular, once broken? Debris from a tree, a pile of feathers and eggshell—nothing moving, except this one thing. It was squishy and pink and it seemed to always have its eyes closed, little beak reaching up and snapping silently at nothing.

Robbie understood that it was an animal—but checking his information banks, did not identify it as any kind of garden pest, and so he did not recognize it. Not knowing why, Robbie bent over to touch the thing.

It flapped harder for a second, tried to flip itself over off its side. Its eyes still closed, Robbie couldn't understand what the creature was trying to do, if it tried to do anything at all. Robbie gave it another poke.

"Vweet!"

Robbie stopped for a second, and lifted his hand.

"Vweeet!! Beeet!"

It kicked up a few tiny footfuls of dirt, scratching on the ground. Robbie still didn't know what to do about it. He searched his memory banks and programming, looking for any hint of what could be done about this pink, fleshy thing. Circuits fired, wires crossed, strings of binary—nothing appropriate came up. What attitude should he adopt? In what way was he meant to regard something like this?

So far out of his experience?

Two wires crossed.

100101011111111111011012

Is that so? Robbie thought.

He didn't know where the idea came from. Somewhere inside him, circuits had come into contact that were not designed to do so, logic gates contradicted each other. CPU interpreting a message it had never processed before.

Robbie bent over the creature a little more gently and cupped it in two hands. It fluttered and contorted in his cool palms, and he walked over towards the tool shed.

Robbie took a rag from a small table in the corner of the shed, spotted with old oil stains, and he curled it up into a comfortable clump. He placed the rag-nest on the table, near the window where the light was still coming in. When that was settled, he placed the naked thing gently down into the center of it.

Robbie watched it try to settle into the clump. It was still visibly uncomfortable, still flapping around, though much less so than when it was lying on the dirt. He took another step back and stared at it for another minute.

100101011111111111011012 made no sense to Robbie on a literal level. It broke the six digit pattern that all of his other functions were mapped to, allowing room for something like ambiguity, multiple conflicting messages.

When Robbie saw the creature, he understood it as *100110, growing—keep safe,* as well as *011001, non-veg—remove from patch.* Robbie did not know what to make of the contradiction—keep safe, disregard. There was nobody who could repair whatever part of him had sent it.

And yet, he had done what was right as well, hadn't he? A new kind of task had come up, and he executed it to the best of his understanding. A growing thing being left to grow, debris removed from

THE GARDENER

the soil. This is what was required of him, wasn't it?

Nobody could have explained to Robbie, nor could he have understood, that it was a random message. He couldn't have been expected to act on it within the bounds of what he'd known.

Robbie looked at the creature for another minute, then returned to his work.

The next morning, the bird was dead. Robbie could not have known that living animals require food or warmth. He was only the gardener. When Robbie went into the shed that morning and saw the twitching thing from yesterday, now still and quiet, he again did not know what to do.

Something to grow, now miscarried. Two circuits fired the sensory input. Something was planted but never harvested, an unborn seed. Procedure *110111* recommends the failed crop be dug up and the soil overturned, but this thing was not buried—it died right there on the table, in the open air with the sun hitting it. What was to be overturned?

Robbie tried harder to understand what he was looking at. Quick, discrete surges of electricity ran through him, equations calculated, input processed. The dead bird would hold his attention until it was made clear what the appropriate response was, how the situation was to be handled. Data run through, information retrieved.

Two wires crossed.

10111010010110111000012

Of course, it could not be more obvious. Robbie faced the dead little bird, stood up straight, and extended his hand.

"Hi, I'm Robbie, your personal gardening assistant. Give me a simple task now such as 'hoe' or 'weed', or consult my manual for inputting a customizable series of errands."

The bird did not respond, it lay there, still very much dead. Robbie was not disappointed, disappointment not being a useful feature for a gardening model, but he was still waiting for a response from someone.

Nobody must be home.

Repeat message.

"Hi," he said again. "I'm Robbie, your personal gardening assistant. Give me Robbie, your 'weed' or consult my Robbie-ie—"

Something came loose inside of him. It had been coming loose for the past several months, but now it had been tilted almost entirely out of its proper socket. Circuits fired, wires crossed. Robbie's speech became slurred, the pre-recorded data from his soundbanks all coming out now, scrambled, making it harder and harder to properly introduce himself to the dead animal.

"Wobbie Sobbie—Hi, I'm simple. Simple inputting a customizable assistant. Give me my manual. Give me my manual. 'hoe'."

"Wobbie Sobbie—"

"Wobbie Sobbie—"

Robbie stood there, arm outstretched, waiting for a handshake. He stuttered and babbled for six hours before finally another component came loose. Whatever initial wires had begun the greeting sequence uncrossed, and Robbie put his arm back down and stopped talking.

Robbie looked around the tool shed. The shadows were steeper, slanting in a different direction than when he had entered. He understood that somehow, in looking at the creature, he had lost half the day. There was no binary string for frustration, it not being a useful condition for a gardening model to have.

Robbie walked over to the other side of the shed, grabbed his hoe, and marched back out to continue his work from yesterday.

*1011101001011011100001*2 puzzled Robbie, inasmuch as he could be puzzled. He continued to think about the bird, and how it ought to be regarded as he gardened in the cooler afternoon sun.

*1011101001011011100001*2 combined the factory default greeting with *disregard, the deregistering of an item from gardening utility—trash.*

Was that what the creature was, then? Trash? If so, why was it so lively before? Other kinds of trash, weeds and empty bags of fertilizer, never kicked and flapped and beeped before needing to be thrown out. And what of the greeting? Why does trash require an introduction?

Robbie finished hoeing the garden, finished the neat lines between the rows by tossing aside a few rocks that had clumped together in the upper-left-hand corner. He was done with the whole length of it, and was now setting the hoe down so that he could go get the watering canister.

The creature was not new to him, or was it? What other reason could one have for introducing themself than if they hadn't met before?

That must be the meaning of 1011101-0010110111000012, he thought. The new thing, the still and quiet skin of the old thing that flapped and made sounds—these two were not the same item. One had replaced the other. It was the only explanation.

Inside, the last few strands of copper wire that kept Robbie's front motion sensor attached to the rest of his processing cortex snapped. He was now getting around with only the front two cameras embedded as his eyes. He did not notice.

Robbie went to go fetch the watering canister, it was dented, and a dull, dirty bronze. This did not affect the quality of water for the crops, so Robbie never attempted to polish it.

"Wobbie Sobbie."

The speaker on top of Robbie's head chimed. He was not consciously using his soundbanks, but the recording went off again.

THE GARDENER

"Wobbie Sobbie."

Robbie looked over at the dead bird one more time, felt *101110100101101110-00012* again, but did not try to introduce himself. Robbie could not feel confused, or low, because those were not useful conditions for a gardening model to exhibit, but he was coming apart on the inside, and there were new ways, he understood, of processing what he saw.

The creature was not plant, but it was also meant to grow, this was *11010220-00101102*. It was also trash, something old to be disregarded, and yet very new, this was *101110100101101110000012*. There were contradictions in what Robbie was seeing, what he was analyzing, and yet they made perfect sense at the same time. His wires were crossed all over, he was beginning to understand this confliction, mishmash of messages. He thought it was very *100111022010120*—the queer hue of an unripe tomato which may be picked anyway, combined with the satisfaction of having planted all of one's seeds for the season—knowing that the success of their growth will be out of one's hands for quite some time now.

Robbie walked over to the table and picked the bird up, out of its oil rag nest and into his hands, clasping one on top of the other.

How strange it had been when it was alive, stranger still now that it wasn't. Robbie did not feel *111000*—the contentment of all crops making it to harvest healthy and whole—but rather *1112001200101*, or perhaps even *110100220001020*—the moment of uprooting a carrot and preparing to classify it as edible or not, mixed with soil analysis after a failed harvest.

Reflection on the past but not for the past's sake, a contentedness in how it could not be avoided.

1112001200101 and *110100220001-020* now combined into a stranger, even more powerful string: *110100220102120-220201*—neither the previous nor the coming harvest is under anyone's control. Only your present moment, and perhaps not even that.

"Wobbie Sobbie."

In the manner of *010101*, Robbie was programmed to take a certain amount of joy, a fulfillment of character in watching growth, but growth is change and change is time and time, was this—

He looked down now. Uncovered the creature with his hand.

000000000001. The dead bird, satisfaction in change, something else in stillness. He had strings of binary and circuits and programming to help him understand something like perfection. Perfection, without the connotation of achievement, without sentiment, is simply fulfillment. Whole in being broken, the bird is finished and perfect.

"Wobbie Sobbie."

000000000001. Robbie put the bird back down, wrapped it up in the oil rag, and took it outside the shed. He carried it to a corner of the garden, just slightly onto the grass, where the soil was still soft, and dug a small hole for it. Robbie placed the bird in the ground and covered it up.

He looked down at his work. The patch of ground where Robbie had decided to place the animal was very obvious, the dirt that piled higher than the rest of the level soil made it clear that something was in there that was not originally so, a permanent fixture of decay.

This too was 000000000001.

Robbie stood back up, and began to walk towards the tool shed. His plastic feet brushed against the clumps of loamy soil that lay to one side or the other of the rows he'd just dug. He did not notice how dirty his feet got, did not notice the debris that lay in front of him. He had only his front two cameras to guide him through the tall grass that stood between him and the tool shed.

Robbie did not notice when he stepped on the handle of his hoe, snapping it in two as his foot came down. Robbie was too wrapped up in 000000000001 now, it was in response to everything. He was able to use the hoe, perfect as it was, even while it was snapped. The wires that had crossed in him, crossed in him, and he no longer needed one string to run into another, one consequence to worry another action.

He simply did what he knew had to be done.

✧

Every morning, Robbie got up and felt 000000000001.

When he watered his garden, every fruit and every vegetable was just as good to eat as any other, because this was an aspect of 000000000001. During the long, dry parts of the year, when no rain came and Robbie was unable to care for his crops properly with just the watering canister, this was also a part of 000000000001.

Robbie saw 000000000001 in everything, and everything was perfect in it.

THE GARDENER

Robbie continued his duties, falling apart slowly as he was, day after day, in and out of years, until one day he found he couldn't stand up. This too was 00000-0000001. For another twelve centuries, he lived off of the sun, his solar panels only needing about two hours of light each day in order for him to operate, and this too was 000000000001.

Wind picked up, knocked over the tool-shed. The grass and weeds grew over his twenty foot by twenty foot garden, making a wild prairie out of his neat rows, but this was also 000000000001. The surface level of the soil rose up, in increments, and each millimeter was a blessing of 0000-00000001. It swallowed his curled up legs first, then his torso. The cameras that were his eyes shut off, and the dirt consumed his chest, shoulders, his face, and finally the top of his head.

When Robbie was no longer able to live off the solar panels embedded on his head, he died. This was 000000000001, and so was everything else.

Every dead bird and deer-eaten radish and crumpled-over tool shed and dented water can and the entire show, all of it was 000000000001.

Laying there. Full.

BETH DAWKINS

THE PULSE OF MEMORY

ORIGINALLY PUBLISHED IN APEX MAGAZINE, JANUARY 2019

The first thing I fell in love with, other than my family, was the fish in tank two. My grandmother, a programmer for the Seasonal Conditions Department, or the SCD, held my hand as she led me off the stone path and away from the mossy green pond. We stepped up to an oak tree that's limbs touched our digital sky.

"Feel this." My grandmother placed my hand against the trunk. The bark was slippery and hard, plastic. Artificial.

My grandmother's smile showed off the ancient lines around her eyes.

"It's a door, little lamb," she explained, stepping to the side of the trunk. She touched the surface and I heard a soft click.

Seamless bark opened. I jumped back and giggled. Electric bulbs flickered on, filling the dark hole with light.

"Where are we going?" I asked, following her down the stairs. I didn't want to go, not at first.

"To show you the fish. You want to see them, don't you?"

The red robes of my grandmother's station, a comfortable reminder of her importance, whispered over her steps. She took my hand as a door slid open at the end of the stairs. The hallway lacked trees and sky, and the air smelled sanitized, like a medical floor. We weren't alone. Adults in important robes of red, blue, and green walked the silver and gray hallway. Translucent holos, like those I played learning games on, hovered in front of their faces.

The hallway curved. Circular windows dotted one side of the wall, providing a view of hundreds and thousands of twinkling stars.

"It's daytime," I said, astonished.

"Yes, but we're in space. Haven't you learned that yet?"

I tried to understand what she meant. Space was empty air and space was outside, filled with darkness and stars.

The tank on the other side of the hallway shimmered under the slanted light from above. Hidden in cloudy aquamarine, dayglow flutters of fluorescents flickered, like starlight. I pressed my hand against the Plexiglas and they moved, danced. Some blinked to an inaudible rhythm and some pulsed.

"What are they?" I whispered.

"Fish," she answered in a matter-of-fact way.

"Cal, has your mother explained death?"

I shook my head, unable to look away.

My grandmother leaned down to my height. I examined the fine lines that creased her neck.

"Before we die, we are put in a tank, not this tank, but a smaller one. The fish take us, our memories, what we've learned and live on until someone eats them. Or they die, consumed by the computers."

"How come?"

"So that nothing is ever lost, lamb." She then pulled me into her arms. "I'll pulse my light for you, forever."

I closed my eyes, breathing in the scent of cooked sugar and earthy dirt. It was the smell of home, the smell of comfort, and love.

✧

Everyone dies at sixty-five. If a soul lives longer their memories risk corruption and are rendered unusable.

History says we lived for much longer until a coming-of-age rite where a boy once ate a bad fish.

The boy was placed in maintenance, on a heating unit. His mistakes caused five deaths and an explosion that fractured society for the next decade. His evaluation proved he had confused the past with the present, due to eroded memories.

The next time I saw the fish was my grandmother's sixty-fifth birthday. Her funeral took place in the glass dome, beside the park. Crowds filled the stands with our family, co-workers in her unit, and old friends. Their heads bowed as they clasped my grandmother's hand. They called her brave as tears fell down their cheeks.

I've heard stories of other grandparents running away from the tank, of being dragged back to the platform, but not my grandmother. She stood tall and erect, calm in her red robes. Music started to play, one of her favorite songs.

Mother gripped my hand. Tears glistened on her cheeks like the stars outside the ship.

Grandmother swayed against the guardrail. Her eyes closed, her head tilted back, and her lips spread up in a smile. The song was old, slow, with lyrics that I couldn't make out. The beat picked up with crashing cymbals and a woman's deep soprano, pouring out one long note of lost romance. The pressure of my mother's grip increased as the song came to an end. I squeaked in protest, shaking my hand out of hers.

The people in the stands murmured as my grandmother stepped away from the tank. And I, like the rest of the gathering, wondered if she might run. She picked up something too small to see and her voice projected through speakers.

"My friends, thank you for seeing me off. It would be harder without you. I've been blessed in life." She paused as if her words had failed her. "I look forward to joining the new generation. Until we meet again."

As she let the tiny microphone drop from her hands she winked at me. My mother moaned and I tried not to smile.

Grandmother walked back down the dock, removing the band that held back her thick mane of gray hair. It wound down in one swift fall. She then unclasped her red robe, letting it tumble down to her feet. She stood before us naked, glorious, and unashamed.

I loved her.

There's nothing so beautiful as that moment of acceptance and surrender. She dove into the tank, graceful and quick. Her form hardly left a ripple on the water's surface. She was obscured until a bright cloud of red spread across the top. It reminded me of her robes, her importance.

Hair, skin, and pieces of her floated to the top. Squirming little bodies started to glow in the clouded water, devouring her.

My mother's cries grew into shrieks as if it was her flesh they'd torn apart.

Little fish flickered pink, flashing and pulsing.

Beautiful.

✧

When the time came to eat my own fish, the ceremony took place in the same glass dome my grandmother had died in. The early morning projection of the sun slipped through the leaves of elm and oak, casting warm yellow rays through the glass. The fluorescent fish shimmered like diamonds under a light, flashing rhythmically, as if in anticipation of being caught. Neon green, hot pink, fuchsia, every color a bright light.

Two families sat in the dome's stands.

A girl, born two hours before me went first. Her family consisted of an older couple, who sat hand-in-hand. In front of them sat a woman with long curly hair, like the girl's. She held onto the back of a little boy's shirt. His hair was just as curly, a shade of dark brown instead of the inky black of his mother's. On the other side of the woman was a man with graying temples. He wore the suit of a watcher, those who kept the peace.

Unlike funeral rites, only family came to the fish consuming.

"No one wants to see teenagers choke down raw fish when they could watch the elderly be dragged to the end of the pool and pushed in," my mom had said. As if it wasn't a privilege to be passed down to the next generation. Her blasphemy could see her arrested if she wasn't careful.

A man in royal blue robes, a "Keeper of Memory," placed a net in the girl's hand. She lifted her head, eyeing her parents in the stands. Her plump bottom lip trembled. Her curls bobbed up and down in time to the sound of her feet on the hard-plastic ground.

The tank gurgled as air bubbles rose to the surface. She dipped the net into the tank, her hand shaking like a tree limb in the park. The net dove deep into the tank and she drew in a sharp breath. She pitched forward, her feet wobbling at the end of the dock.

I wondered what would happen if she fell in. Would her blood blossom up, turning the water from blue-green to a red cloud?

Her hand shot up with the net, a wiggling fish pulsing with purple light caught in the mesh. The Keeper removed the fish from the net and with practiced ease he slit the bottom of the fish open. Blood trickled out and landed at his feet as he scooped out the glistening entrails and dropped them into the water. Glowing fish broke the surface of the water, devouring the insides of their doomed sibling.

The girl was handed the fish. It was expected that she would eat as much as she could stomach. Her plump lips thinned and she grew pale. She bit into the side of the fish, choking and sputtering on the raw meat. Iridescent scales clung to the sides of her mouth and cheeks.

The Keeper offered her water before she could heave the fishy morsels up. She coughed into it, drinking her fill, before she took another bite. Her lips turned red with the fish's blood, as she swallowed, choking it down.

My stomach turned, disgusted by her dishonor. Each bite gave her a piece of our history. Each bite held her future.

My Gran's hands and voice had not trembled as she dove into the future.

I set my sights on the yellow and white ones. Council members wore robes of white. Yellow was for the engineers. I didn't know if the color of the fish bore any real significance, but I was willing to hope.

Another Keeper helped the girl off the platform, offering her a cloth napkin.

"Can we go home now, Mommy?" the little boy in the stands asked.

"Cal," my mother cried. Tears slid down her cheeks as they had for my grandmother.

"Don't cry," I told her as the Keeper handed me the net.

My palm was sweaty on the handle. I gripped it tighter and climbed onto the dock. Fluorescent dots twinkled under my feet, like a sea of stars. My mouth watered in anticipation. They'd taste like power and promise, each and every one.

I've never understood how memories go from a fluorescent glow and translate into static thoughts and information. It's been explained through enzymes in the stomach and digestive tract, to blood cells and how our bodies absorb vitamins. The fish absorb calcium when they devour us, along with memories, causing the glow. It's called Photoprotein. The glow lets us know it's working. Our people broke down the steps and engineered the fish to need us, and in turn, we needed them. It's a giant circle that's traced back into the computer, keeping our existence regulated, making sure nothing is ever wasted.

There was other edible marine life, but none that could be genetically modified to contain our souls.

The Keeper muttered directions to me, but I didn't listen. I leaned down and waited for the flicker of a yellow or white one. To my right I saw it. I dipped the net down, scooping colors in as if I'd done it hundreds of times.

Three little bodies wriggled in my net, splashing, and tossing. A purple one jumped out, its body twisted in the air, flinging tiny droplets of water across my face.

The Keeper laughed beside me and took the net.

"Blue or yellow? It's rare to have a choice," he said.

"Yellow," I answered.

He tossed the blue back in with a plop. The small yellow one wiggled in his grip. The Keeper removed a knife from his robes and the digital sunlight cast reflections off its metallic surface. He carved out the innards of the fish's belly, and I held in a protest.

I wanted it whole.

He handed me the fish and I sucked out its eyes, popping them between my teeth as if they were a rare delicacy. The gelatinous mixture was both sweet and salty. I crunched on the rubbery insides, below the gills. It tasted like salt and undercooked meat. Blood trickled down the sides of my mouth as I bit into the blood vessel along the backbone. I licked the sides of my mouth and ran my fingers under the sharp bones for the tender meat that melted on my tongue.

The Keeper's hands gathered in front of him like a proud father, his eyes ablaze with false sunlight.

My mother gasped from the stands.

The girl who had eaten her fish before stood at the exit, watching. Her gaze held mine as I stripped the last fibers of meat from the bones and savored the moment they slid down my gullet.

✧

The first real memory that surfaced happened in a dream. In the dream I worked at my terminal: code, code, and more code. Davey came over with his sheet of ones and zeros. His breath smelled like decay, and all I wanted to do was go home and have a giant glass of wine.

I glanced back at the tiny zeros and ones and tried to see what he pointed at and then realized he wasn't looking at the sheet. He was looking at my tits.

"Christ, Davey!" I snatched the paper out of his hand and he was gone.

He was gone and I wasn't at work.

I stood next to a chubby-cheeked boy with black hair and blacker eyes. He pointed out to sea. A ship sailed over water that reflected the blanket of tiny stars above. I handed the paper to the little boy, who laughed and said, "We'll sail a new ocean. You'll see, Calvin."

"Calvin, sweetheart?"

I opened my eyes to mother's hand on my shoulder, and her face, tearless for once, hovered over me. She sat down on the edge of my bed when I gripped the soft foam blanket tighter to my chest. I wanted to press my hand against my chest, to make sure I wasn't the woman I dreamed.

"Did you have one of the dreams, already?" Mom asked. She smelled like strawberries and nail polish.

I cleared my throat and thought of the sea, which wasn't a sea at all, but space that expanded infinitely outside of our ship. I'd known those things but not how to read a galactic map.

The little boy in my dream, his name was Puash, a child prodigy and scientist. He'd recorded maps, hundreds of maps.

He wasn't the only memory. The one before him, a borderline alcoholic, Crystal, was an old-world coder. She was the oldest memory the fish had given me. She'd lived half of her life on Earth, in the Before.

I bobbed my head up and down. "The Before," I said to my mother as she gripped my hand.

"I have one of those," mother said.

She used to work on the medical floor, but she hadn't worked since my father had fallen ill. He received a grave diagnosis and was given to the fish shortly after.

I was too young to remember.

"I'm not supposed to talk about it," I said.

She didn't nod her head or tell me it was okay. Instead, she let go of my hand and straightened the lampshade. "Just remember, they're not us. Just memories."

I closed my eyes and imagined the wink my grandmother gave me, right before she dove in.

The fish held the doors to the past and our final dive into the unknown.

✧

When I submitted my placement test, I was named an assistant Keeper of Memory. My robes were aquamarine.

A Keeper of Memory's duties were to take care of the conveyor of memories, the fish. My memories were full of coding, star maps, and maintenance level work, but the test singled me out for blue robes. I cleaned the tanks and monitored the proteins in the water. Senior members, starting at age forty-five, administered placement tests and prepared the ceremonies. Three weeks, after two coming-of-age rites and cleaning out more tanks than I could count, I took my second fish.

The impulse came in the evening as I watched over one of the tanks where I believed my grandmother's fish throbbed neon pink. I'd dimmed the lights so that the water shone silver and black in the low light. Tiny lights sparkled in the depths and I connected the dots creating ever-shifting maps to far away star systems.

I took up a net and stepped toward the feeding plank. The tank was larger and deeper than the pool used for coming-of-age rites and memory acquisition. It held the bulk of the fish old enough and large enough for human consumption.

I scooped a fluorescent pink fish into my net. It squirmed and wiggled, protesting the fate of my teeth.

I thought of the story of the young man who'd eaten corrupted data, and then I saw my grandmother—naked as the day she was born.

She'd promised to see us again.

The fish squirmed in my grip. I bit into its gills before I lost my grip. The spiny ray above the dorsal fin cut into my palm. Our blood mixed and slid down my hands as slippery scales came off in my mouth.

I threw the innards into the tank and munched on the soft meat along tiny bones. I pierced the large blood vessel and sucked at it until my head spun. I sucked at the eyes last, savoring the delicate flavor that burst across my tongue.

I'd washed, changed, and sat down in the locker room, half regretting what I'd done.

And then memories ripped through me.

On a school trip we'd explored a menagerie of Earth's animals locked away in enclosures. Great hunting cats lounged under warming lamps, licking their giant claws. I'd wanted to see those claws tearing into the flesh of their prey.

The memories tore through me like giant claws. Great talons gouging my skull, filling it with flashes of pain and memories. Attaching electrodes and sending pulses into my temples would've been kinder. I ground my teeth together as I became more.

I saw an old man in a hospital bed—the oldest man I'd ever seen. Machines beeped, standing alongside tubes that connected to catheters. The old man gripped my hand and squeezed. "You can't let them go through with this. You can't let them stick me in that tank. You know it isn't right!"

He was too old to go in a tank, but this was before the rule of sixty-five.

"They'll sedate you first. You wanted this," I told him, angry that he was backing out. He'd die either way, but this way some of him would stay behind.

I wasn't scared of death, and I tried to remind myself that it was easier to think that with so many good years left.

Only I didn't think it. She did.

"Dammit, Layla! Would you just listen?" the old man asked.

The words were in French, from the Before.

I blinked, and I was Cal again.

✧

I scrubbed the tank with a long brush and thought of Layla. Her memories were sharper than the others.

I watched the tank holo apps as I worked. One of the app's readings spiked—a drop in the water temperature from tank three. The tank housed what we called, "The Hungry Fish." Their translucent bodies were pale white, the color of steam. They wouldn't hold the memories of devoured souls until they reached maturity.

I logged in and sent the readout to the tank system administrator and my manager. I headed down the spiral staircase to the tank's environmental control unit. Fish occasionally appeared beside the unit from within, their ghostly visage dancing in the dark water.

A yellow notification flashed in the corner of my eye. I opened it and the administrator said, "Try manually shutting it down and then start it back up. If that doesn't fix the problem, let me know."

Why I hadn't made administrator yet was a mystery, not when their job revolved around common sense.

I shut the unit down and waited for the humming to die.

Green and blue fish in the tank behind me huddled together in threes and fours.

I turned back on the unit and waited for the hum to stabilize.

I eyed the fish that followed me. My mouth watered as I imagined sucking their eyes out.

The fish I took was electric green, brighter than our genetically-enhanced trees. I bit into it as the temperature in tank three returned to normal.

✧

"Ugh. Why are we still in bed?" asked Layla, the French biologist.

She was me. I was her, and there was no line in-between, not after the last fish.

"Just a few more minutes," Puash, the boy, said as I rolled over.

I was a child genius. Who did I need to get up for?

I knew the voices weren't real. Only they were real, years ago they had lives, and now I made them real again. This wasn't supposed to be how souls lived on.

It could be a side effect. Too many souls trapped in my brain tissue. Layla reminded me that wasn't how the fish worked.

Memories weren't souls. Souls were for the religious and spiritual. But she wasn't certain about anything.

The boy flickered back and forth. He thought work was boring, and he hated my apartment.

The strongest persona, stronger than Layla, called herself Repair. Her memories were sharp wrong things that drove nails into the sides of my head as if she were fighting me.

In the ship year 204, she'd been the captain's wife, until she led a rebellion against the council and her captain.

She should have been fed to the computer, not the fish.

Her rebellion ended in the park by the same tree that my grandmother had led me into. A shootout involving stun grenades and tranquilizer guns haunted my dreams. I could feel the beat of her heart and the sweat on her forehead.

"We have to split up and go around," she'd said to her meager group of ten.

Men and women bobbed their heads and their stolen weapons flashed silver under an artificial sunset. She knew they were all done for, but if she could find a place to hide the chip...

The chip, hidden in a necklace shaped as Thor's hammer, Mjölnir, rested against her chest. Her squad fanned out, drawing fire long enough to hide the chip in a stone beside the doorway. She opened the tree door with a soft click before pain

shot through her back. The dart stung, wrapping her body in cold fear as she fell and fell.

"We have to see if the chip is still there. We can still end this," Repair urged me.

"End what?" I demanded, standing under my living unit's shower head.

"The fish." It wasn't Repair that said it, but Layla.

I laughed at them and thought of my fluorescent stars, my tiny sweet bodies. As if I'd ever destroy them.

And then I wasn't in the shower anymore. I was a tied up ten-year-old boy. His arms were bound above his head. The crane lifted Puash—me—above the ground until my feet dangled in empty air. My shoulders throbbed. The crane moved over a pool where little ghost bodies swam in inky black water.

Momma would come. Momma wouldn't let this happen to me. Where was she?

The crane started to lower and his feet (my feet) came closer and closer to the water below.

"Dammit. Stop!" I screamed at all of them, but others were giving their death stories.

Repair didn't know hers, nor did Layla, but there were others. A man who'd never see his daughters grow or see his grandchildren. Another woman who'd just found love, real love. The kind that filled her heart and made her knees weak. A week later she turned sixty-five. Her lover promised her that he'd watch her last moments, and she promised him that his face would be the last thing she'd ever see, but that hadn't happened. It'd been the whip-thin man in blue robes. He pushed her off the dock, his lips pulled back in a cruel smile.

"How many years before it's your mother?" Layla and Repair asked together, in two different languages.

A message shut them all up. A message in red. It wasn't from my contact list, but whoever had sent it was important enough to escape my blocker. It was an assistant member of the council asking to meet.

Another message, this one in yellow, from my manager. He wanted to let me know I had the day off at the formal request of the council.

"They're going to kill you, too. Get the chip before that happens," said Repair.

"What's on the chip?"

Silence answered, but her frustration buried itself in my skin and tingled in my fingertips.

Either the council wanted the chip and knew what voices warred in my head or I was going to get dropped in the tank. All life goes to the fish and back into humanity. And if not humanity then to the computer. Nothing ever really dies, not in space.

"That's a lie!" the boy screamed.

My fist struck the counter. My knuckles throbbed. I hadn't hit the counter. It was the little boy who could chart the universe. The rebels in my head drowned me out.

Repair hit the button to open my door.

Repair took over my body as my vision blurred and narrowed. My feet ran down the steel stairs, headed toward the shuttle.

I was her.

White walls blurred into gray slants that dimmed to darker shadows.

"This is death for us," whispered one of the others.

"If you consume us, then you are us. How much better would it be if you could have kept your grandmother a while longer?" asked Layla.

"What is Repair doing?" I asked.

"What she has to," said the man who never got to see his little girls grow up. Every single person in my head agreed.

Did my grandmother feel this way? Was she floating in someone's head, telling them that consuming her was wrong?

"The killing is wrong," Layla snapped. "Why don't you get it? The government takes life and uploads it into children. Why, Cal? Because it's easier than teaching them how to do their jobs?"

"But no one really dies and nothing is ever really lost," I argued. We're gods conserving the heavens inside of us.

The voices stopped and I could see again. I stood under the artificial tree in the park my grandmother took me to as a child. The sky was soft blue with puffy clouds that lazily crossed the sun. A small stream bubbled up from the rocks and ran along the trail.

"Well?" asked a woman behind me, only she wasn't a woman.

She, like me, was seventeen cycles. The girl who had eaten a fish before me at the coming-of-age rite. Her robes were pressed, white, and embroidered silver and gold along the hem. The robes identified her as an assistant to the council.

A message popped up in yellow. My presence was demanded before council chambers. A clerk, not an assistant, had sent it. Behind the girl stood her father.

"You asked me here," I said, surprised. "Not the council."

"I'll ask you one more time, or you can deal with my father. Where is the chip?"

Her father held something black that pointed at me, a stunner.

"If they knew what I did, they'll know what you're about to do," I warned her, backing up toward the tree.

"No. We made sure of that. And we know the repair virus has infected you," she said.

My back touched the tree door. Its solid structure was the only thing that kept me from the stairs. I'd rather be replanted in someone's skull than at the mercy of whatever this girl was part of.

"Repair virus?" I asked. She smirked, her lips drawing back to expose teeth as white as her robe.

"You've met her already."

My hand pressed the tree door. It clicked as her meaning became clear. Repair was never the wife of a captain. She was a virus and I was infected.

"The chip, now," she said.

The chip was a step away from me, if it was still hidden in the rock, but if the memory of Repair was fake then why would the chip be there at all?

I threw the door open and rushed down the same stairs my grandmother led me down once. The girl's father chased me. His boots pounded the stairs matching my heartbeat.

"I knew your grandmother, Cal," he called.

No. My grandmother had seen her fate in blue waters. She'd dove in, head first without blinking.

"She helped us engineer the virus, using her DNA. That chip is the next step, the test that means you're ready."

A hundred fish had pulsed in a dark tank, like gemstones, waiting to be worn. Waiting to be reborn. My grandmother had leaned down beside me, her robes whispering against the floor.

So that nothing is ever lost, she'd said.

Angry heat rose inside my chest like a wave crashing. I whipped around, facing my attacker.

"Liar," I accused, like a curse, spraying spittle. "She'd never help you."

The stun rod in the watcher's hands didn't look the same. The tip was red, like the color of water after the fish ate.

"It's a shame, Cal. You're turning her sacrifice into nothing."

My grandmother smiled at her end.

I forced my lips up and eyed him. He laughed, as if I was some sort of joke, and then the dark wand jabbed my chest.

"Did you get him?" asked the girl, through a holo app.

"Yes. He's gone. We'll have to wait till the next program goes active."

Warmth gave way to heat as if flames ate my insides. Orange and then yellow circles crowded my vision. In their bright centers I found darkness. It reached out and consumed everything. The fire inside of my skin left my arms numb, followed by my legs. I could hear a high pitch whine.

I'll pulse my light for you, forever, my grandmother had said.

I'd thought she knew how glorious the souls were, floating as if angels in a sky. I reached out, with arms made of thoughts. I tried to call out to her but I had no mouth, no arms. I was nothing.

As life turned its back on me, I wanted more time. Seventeen wasn't enough, neither was sixty-five.

"We are here," said the boy.

Together we hummed a lullaby that my Grandmother had sung to me. Before we faded, I saw a flicker of hot-pink light.

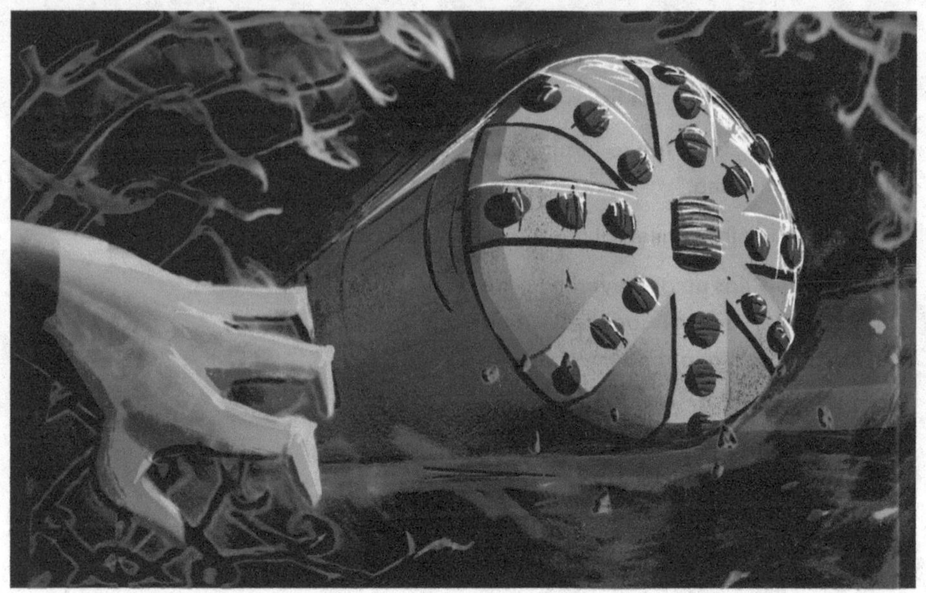

SARA SAAB

BURROWING MACHINES

ORIGINALLY PUBLISHED IN THE DARK, JANUARY 2019

There was a strange agitation to London that summer from the very beginning, a hormonal moodiness; a belly heat, if cities could be said to go through such things. We had enough sunshine to roll around in, but twilight snapped to dark between one sentence and the next, like someone had tossed a quilt over the giant lamp of the sun.

They had found all those new fossils while digging up the duck pond at Hampstead Heath and they shut the footpath the whole way round. People like me, who were barely getting themselves out the door for a jog in the park in the late afternoon haze, gave up on exercise entirely.

By May, I was sleeping from the end of my night shift all the way through to my final cut-the-bullshit alarm at 8pm. I'd crawl out of bed feeling like death warmed up. I'd put on my orange hi-viz and cargoes, and a stripe of lipstick, God knows who for, and walk down to Camden Town Station with my hard hat's suspensions pushing against the blood-beat of a head-ache at my temples.

The drilling work in the tunnel, at least, started miraculously on schedule. I lost myself for underground hours that summer planning the reroute of London's Victorian water mains around the burrowing machines' trajectory, the construction of temporary wall struts and the boring of holes for soil samples.

I spent most of my waking hours fifteen meters below ground in a dark punctuated by machine headlights, flashlight beams, and shadows, and on the rare occasions I met Adarsh at the Old Man's Arms for a fish supper and a dry cider before work, he'd give me that look that told me he thought I was in urgent need of rescue from my life.

"No one but you would be this into burrowing, Jo," he said when I met him in early June.

"We haven't had a new tunnel for the Northern Line in three decades," I reminded him around a tartar-sauced chunk of battered cod.

"How filthy is that dirt you're shoveling anyway? All London's millennia of shite, and bones, and bubonic plague, and more shite."

"It doesn't bother me. If you saw these giant tunneling machines do what they do, I think you'd appreciate it."

Adarsh sipped his craft ale, eyebrows high enough on his forehead that they almost skimmed his turban.

"And you hear the river through some of the walls," I added.

"The Thames?"

"No, you numpty. The River Fleet."

"The underground stream."

Adarsh poked a stuffed olive with a toothpick. Made me think of Fran, who'd hated all foods that didn't belong in sandwich bread.

"Proper river. High and low tides. Currents. Everything. At high tide it vibrates in the stone."

The River Fleet—London's geologic minotaur, winding North to South, fallen out of favor, diminished and trapped underground in its labyrinth of sewers back in the eighteenth century. The tourist-friendly experience was the faint hush of it through a tiny sewer grate on Ray Street in Clerkenwell. Being separated from the Fleet by just an underground tunnel wall in the small hours of morning was an entirely different thing.

But that was just trivia.

None of it would matter until later.

In late June, we started to slip behind on the tunnel expansion project. When I looked at Annabel's Gantt charts, it all seemed minor—engineers taking unexplained sick days, a pervasive anxiety that stretched ten-minute breaks to twenty. Like that same out-of-sortsness that had been weighing on me was spreading.

The first really observably weird thing happened on a Saturday night, two hours after the last Northern Line train. We were doing a tunnel walkthrough when one of our junior engineers, Philip, noticed a hole punched in the wall of the existing southbound Tube tunnel.

Grey moon rocks of concrete and a pile of dust dampened in the maintenance crawlspace beside the train tracks. We stuck our flashlights through the hole, wide as a crockpot, to the void on the other side. Our beams spotlighted the adjoining space. Glaze and slime on old brickwork. Water babbled along well below the level of the hole.

"I didn't know the Fleet flowed right alongside here," Philip said, and ran a hand round the hole's ragged edge. "That's maybe half a meter of concrete."

"Are there burrowing machines on the other side? In the Thames Water tunnels?" I asked no one in particular. I knew there weren't. There shouldn't be.

"Nah," said Philip.

"Structural weakness," I said. But the concrete around the hole was sound. No sagging, no hairline cracks, no subsidence.

What it looked like to me? Like someone had battered through the tunnel wall-- from the River Fleet's adjoining tunnel, into ours.

✧

They filed a police report and launched the obligatory Health and Safety investigation, but by mid-July, nothing. After another week, Thames Water's guys patched up the hole. We bolted in some steel mesh to reinforce the concrete along that segment of the Northern Line.

The tunnel expansion was finding its feet again. We had a thirty-meter span of freshly excavated tunnel that we could walk into upright, arms outstretched, and more importantly, we hadn't burst a single Thames Water pipe under my watch.

Privately, I tried to adjust myself out of my funk.

Adarsh talked me into a deal on twenty hot yoga passes at a studio in Chalk Farm. I stupidly showed up for the first lesson in tracksuit bottoms and a cotton sweater (Adarsh hadn't told me what hot yoga was) and left so dehydrated, I barely went to the loo for two days. I gave Adarsh nineteen passes back. Then I got together with his friend Aman a few time—awkward daytime rendezvous because of my flipped schedule. I bought myself an urban spa retreat, booked a week off in autumn, signed up for a wine delivery service. Cheap screw-top bottles of picpoul. The crates took over my tiny kitchen, but what do you do.

Did it help? I thought so. I did. I felt cared for, if only by my own self. But the world wasn't done with me, and neither was my brain.

So, I suppose, first, the dreams. About Fran. Dream-Fran. Fish-Fran.

That July, she turned up night after night, carrying the blue fishing rod, our Christmas gift to our father, the one I'd been toying with when she wandered off. Glossy as a brand-new car, that rod, and I can still see the polish of it nearly three decades on. In dream-Fran's other hand was the tin bucket we used for treasure

BURROWING MACHINES

unearthed on our mudlarking adventures along the bank of the Thames.

When I remember my sister, I remember her with her braids and wellies, her missing teeth. But dream-Fran wasn't like that. She was indistinct—not like she'd been rubbed out or sun-faded, but sort of like she was made of squid skin. Her eyes were black dots in jelly flesh, her nose two upward punctures you'd miss if you weren't looking. The bucket and rod were what tipped me off that it was her.

Fish-Fran didn't do anything in the dreams, just hung around me. I couldn't see where we were exactly, but it felt like we were in the tunnels, that same cozy swaddled feeling and layering of shadows.

"Where did you go?" I asked her, every night.

"I went to find the mouth of the Thames that daddy talked about," she said, or, "I was hunting for rubies and sapphires in the mud," or, "I went to look for something important in the water."

"Are you alive?" I asked her.

But instead of assortments of answers, I got nothing—or once, the touch of her jelly skin on mine.

London is so rammed with stories it's hard to connect the dots across the width and depth of it. But now that I've pieced it all together, something else happened in July, the first clue to really hang onto.

A piece of a puzzle no one wanted to see completed.

The fossils from Hampstead Heath went to the paleontologists. They measured and prodded them and said: an ancient organism, amphibious, big, really big. We don't have a name for it yet.

Anyway. That's what there was.

Dad had let us fish with the glossy blue rod, but said we couldn't eat anything we caught in the Thames: too sickly, too poisoned. Throw it back, he'd say.

London and its millennia of shite and history, like Adarsh said.

On the night of Saturday July 23rd, the red LED of the station clock showing a half hour to midnight, I was an endless up-escalator away from both the trains and engineering crew, chatting to the station supervisor in the ticket hall over a cup of Darjeeling and a pack of chocolate digestives. It was some banter about the new line, how convenient it would be to have a direct route from Camden Town to Luton Airport once our work was done.

There was a slight rumbling beneath my work boots and then a metallic scraping sound. More rumbling. A short time later a ruffled announcement rang out on the tannoy: "Inspector Sands to Northern Line southbound platform four."

Inspector Sands: code for emergency at a Tube station, among Londoners an open secret. We were already on the escalator, taking steps as nimbly as our boots would allow, my stomach a bony fist.

Downstairs, pandemonium.

It was the last southbound service on a Saturday night. Drunk passengers hammered wildly on the windows of the train from within and from out on the platform; its doors were still closed. The train driver had abandoned her cab, was shouting *I don't know* at the platform supervisor, then, louder, at the station supervisor who arrived along with me.

Below the periodic shattering of glass, under blows of the train's emergency escape hammers, there was a sound like a faint waterfall, and a stench like a swamp. The waterfall noise was loudest at the dark maw of the tunnel, where the train had been holding at a red signal.

The rails flooded in a minute.

Grey water began to rise toward platform level. We had engineering crews, not far away reviewing plans and prepping the night's work, as well as passengers onboard the stricken train. There weren't enough people at that time of night for a crush, but I remember a lot of panicked milling and a nervous kind of shouting that reminded me of the animal pens at my aunt Calista's dairy farm. After we got the train's doors open, we focused on the most critical thing: getting everybody the hell out of the station.

Upstairs, after every passenger had been evacuated and emergency services had arrived, it was Philip who was first to realize it.

"Jo, can I talk to you for a minute?"

He pulled me aside.

"Hopefully I'm all muddled up, okay? But that was a nine-car service. The last service is always nine cars. I left the excavation as soon as I heard it. Ran down to see. Counted the carriages." He counted idly on his fingers now, hesitated on the second set of five. "The eighth carriage I could see was still sort of in the tunnel. It hadn't come all the way out, and it was dark behind."

Philip could barely look at me. There was an awful look in his eyes—a burden I could tell he was about to pass to me, a live grenade.

"There were only eight. Only eight cars."

"Where was the ninth?"

Philip shook his head. He was two years out of apprenticeship, a competent, honest kid from South London whose mother had forced him into the vocational program when all he wanted was to record drill albums and chase his sliver of fame from club to club.

"No ninth carriage back there, Jo," he said. "Just water and stink and fucking darkness."

Within a week there were names and pictures: fifteen souls who had made the mistake of choosing the wrong carriage, the wrong train, the wrong bloody night. I scrolled past the news story because I couldn't look at their faces. Most were university students; there were two cousins on a stag night; a pensioner coming back from the theatre with his grandson.

There was a protracted search: divers, the Fire Brigade, the daily press briefings. They would keep looking, they said. They wouldn't give up. But they found nothing.

The ninth carriage had disappeared.

The Northern Line was out of service citywide, our worksite off-limits. I made sure to take no pleasure from rejoining the world of the living. I barricaded myself in bed with the curtains drawn and experimented with sleeping pills that would stop me from dreaming of fish-Fran.

Adarsh called enough times that I switched my mobile off. I didn't have the stomach for him, for anyone. Or, not quite: I would have talked to my father if he were still alive. I would have done anything to speak to him.

Another week and an emergency dam was put into the River Fleet's tunnel. This allowed an engineering team—thankfully not mine—to drain the southbound Northern Line track.

In early August, they'd drained enough water and shifted enough rubble that they found the hole.

It was massive, a breach tall and wide as a Routemaster. It was in the same section as the last hole, an implosion of concrete that'd torn through our mockery of a reinforcement mesh like a tongue through a sheet of tissue. Measurements confirmed the hole was well big enough to let through a train carriage, if you could get around the logistics of a twenty-five ton block of metal detaching from train and track and maneuvering through to a parallel tunnel.

The search operation scoured as much of the underground river as it could. And found nothing. All of London turned its attention to the River Thames, especially where the Fleet let out into its postcard-perfect sibling through the embankment wall beneath Blackfriars Bridge.

"How can a whole train car of people go missing underground?" asked Adarsh, when he'd insisted on a fish supper enough times that I had to oblige or risk him attempting some kind of intervention.

"I don't know." Speech tasted wooden. I couldn't touch my dinner and nursed a double vodka soda, even though the late daylight was obscenely cheerful. "It doesn't make sense."

But of course, I speculated—all I did lately was speculate—trying out ideas too laced with impossibility to be anything but thoughts I had in private. I wondered how many of us had made the same leap, sensed the same wrongness about the city in spite of the smiling glare of its streets.

I wondered what we'd upset. What history we'd woken.

✦

No brand of sleeping pills was strong enough to make Fran go away.

By the muggy middle of August I was becoming accustomed to her following me around the subterranean tunnels of my dream world.

"Where are we going, Jo?" she asked one night in her five-year-old voice, skipping ahead of me down a tunnel. The flash-lit shadow of the fishing rod extending long and black and hook-ended before her.

"Anywhere. Shall we go and find you?"

She reached a grey, oozing hand toward me. "I'm right here."

"And other times?" I asked. "Where are you when I'm awake?"

"I'm nowhere there. I don't live there. It's too wet." I took my sister's hand. We walked side by side. The feel of her repulsed me, but I clung to my memory of real Fran as hard as I could.

"And I like swimming, but not that kind of swimming," said Fran.

"What kind of swimming?" I asked. The tunnel was tight. My shoulders scraped wet brick.

"Swimming until you can't see London Bridge Is Falling Down. Till you can't see Jo or Daddy. Swimming until you get hurt."

"But there's none of that bad swimming now," I said.

Fran stopped. She set down the mud-larking bucket and put steamed-dumpling fingers to the damp wall of the tunnel.

"Yes there is, Jo. I feel it. It's back. You and daddy can't make it go away."

"Can you?" I asked.

"No," said Fran, in a singsong. "Nobody can."

✧

We went back to work on the tunnel that week. It was almost too somber to bear. Not a single joke, not a sloppy innuendo, not a crack about the weather, not even the reliable no-daylight vampire analogy. Not once. But the vibrations of the burrowing machines still soothed me, I suppose. I felt more myself than I had in a long time.

The project was two months behind, but no one mentioned it. Not even Annabel-of-the-Gantt-charts dared breathe a word about deadlines after what happened.

And late was better than never. Our fresh thirty-meter excavation was soon double that. We were doing good work.

One night we got a little careless, detonated a badly calibrated blasting emulsion to loosen stubborn bedrock too close to the soft side wall. And we had on our hands another breach between Tube tunnel and river tunnel, this time a small one, fist-sized, likely harmless.

Philip brought me over to assess the damage.

"The Fleet must be at low tide," I said.

"How do you want to fix it?" he asked.

"I reckon cement, this time," I said.

Ancient brickwork on the Fleet's side had been damaged by the blast, chunks of it missing. There was a peephole gap clear through. I put my ear against it as if it were a subterranean conch shell.

The dirge of the buried river, soft and insistently there.

"Jo?"

"Go get the drilling crew and Thames Water's engineer, please."

"Yes boss."

Philip's flashlight beam bounced away toward the mouth of the excavation. I was alone.

I knelt in front of the breach, waterlogged rock and silt cool against the padded knees of my cargoes.

I can't describe why I got so close. I felt turned around, turned upside down, like the furniture of my life was hanging from the ceiling. I wanted to sleep in the sunshine and rave all night. Wanted to compress London to a snow globe, then to a point. Wanted to swim in the Thames and take that impure brown water into my lungs.

There was dripping and burbling and my breathing overtop, a symphony.

I shone my flashlight through. On the other side, a blinding, slick, prismatic reflection, no depth. Bulk, right up close.

I took a work glove off. And I touched. Felt the give and muscle of an enormous living thing.

I suppose all stories are passed along with cheap words, tinsel and streamers. I know there's nothing I can really say. And maybe the moment you touch a monster and don't draw back is the moment you become one, molt your humanity.

But I'd never felt so old and I'd never felt so buried alive. The expanses and alleys and green spaces of London were at that moment barely pockets of oxygen, barely enough for a day's survival in a very, very long life. And then it was gone. And Philip was back.

"You probably have this under control," I said, because I didn't, and hurried toward the industrious snake of the up-escalator, my body a bundle of broomsticks wrapped in leather.

✧

We completed the tunnel in autumn of the following year. I attended the ribbon cutting ceremony for the new Northern Line service—Camden Town to Luton Airport—in a pinstripe jacket and pencil skirt that I'd dry-cleaned for the occasion. They stood me somewhere near the back, which was fine by me. I'd been offered a plus-one but I didn't invite Adarsh. I wanted to be there by myself.

Then, around Christmas, under a frosted Blackfriars Bridge, curls of metal chassis still glossy with the livery of a Northern Line train began to let out into the Thames where the mouth of the Fleet was. They ran dragnets at the outlet for a month or more.

No human remains were recovered.

Around the same time a new species of amphibian was discovered in the shallows of the Thames. The Royal Society wanked and self-congratulated for weeks. The specimens were thought to be juveniles, or, crazy as it sounded, larvae. They were proper big babies, long as a human arm.

The tabloids published an exposé, all of them printing the same pixelated photo of an alleged specimen alongside a strip of measuring tape. It had hundreds of needle teeth and kind of sad, mopey, monochrome eyes and a keratin knob on its forehead and—most importantly—what appeared to be the yellow strap of a carriage handle embedded in its eel-like, translucent flesh. But tabloids are tabloids, and London is chock full of stories. So people forget.

Oh, and the fossils in the duck pond of Hampstead Heath had a name now. They called the prehistoric beast the Dendan, after a mythical fish in the Arabian Nights. Said it was likely king of the aquatic food chain in its time, being bigger than a galleon, with a carnivore's teeth and a stomach the size of a hotel room. A good one. A penthouse suite.

You'd think more people would have made the connection. Maybe I find it easier to believe impossibilities than others do. I don't know.

I climbed out of my funk, little by little. The dreams mostly stopped. I like to think Fran had told me all I needed to know.

Now, when I think about our terrible last day with Fran on the bank of the Thames, I can't help but see it differently. Less like me being distracted and losing my little sister when our father went to fetch a pail of bait from the car. Less like her being picked up by a dirty and depraved pervert. More like Fran seeing the prismatic writhe of fish in the shallows, wading out to try to catch one, or to play.

I force myself to imagine it was quick after that, the bad swimming, the hurt.

Anyway, it's all guesswork and fantasy. I don't see the harm in building a sand fortress that protects your heart a little better.

That's that. They asked me to work on the eastbound expansion of the Central Line, but I said no thanks. I enrolled in a paleozoology diploma course. Lectures at 9am every other day.

I'd forgotten how frantic London is during rush hour, how many lives there are to be shuttled along its roads and its bridges and tunnels. Deaths, births, seasons.

How many stories the city can absorb like a sponge.

ANDREW GIFFIN

REPTILIAN BARBARIAN AND THE TEMPLUM SOLARIUM

The crone's laughter drifted out of Yix's satchel, where he kept her severed head. He ignored her, focusing on the howling of the wind across the rocky highlands. Her laugh pierced his ear like a knife across glass. He bent to one knee and swung the leather bag from his shoulder.

Dirt battered his face, and he squinted one set of eyelids against the tiny wind-borne missiles. He loosened the drawstring and opened the bag. Her head lay at the bottom, face toward the sky, her mouth a cruel smile.

She laughed louder as her milky white eyes searched blindly.

"You march toward your death, betrayer. Murderer."

She let out another horrible laugh.

"Death comes to the lucky ones, hag. You don't understand because it will never find you, but I don't fear it."

Yix shoved a rag in her mouth, tying it with a length of twine. She screamed, the sound muffled. Her face twisted in hatred as Yix pulled the bag shut and swung it back over his shoulder. He used his ax to help him stand, the blade still covered in her melted body.

As he resumed his climb, Yix's mind turned to memories of Zoh. *I will be with you again soon, my love.*

Yix had tracked down the crone two days earlier. Rumors of a seer in the depths of the Smog Flats were true, it seemed. The fog of the swamp followed him inside her dimly lit hut, mixing with candle smoke. There was no smell. This should have been a relief considering the stink outside, but the emptiness disturbed him instead.

She sat against the far wall. Her white eyes glowed in the darkness, and a shiver ran down his scales as they passed sightlessly over him. She was one of the Boto, the metal people.

Her voice creaked like a rusted gate. "Who enters? Speak, wretched worm! Come to steal from a helpless old woman?"

He sneered at her performance. "You are no old woman, and you're certainly not helpless."

Surprise passed across her wizened face before her mouth cracked open in a smile. She let out a cackle, and Yix's blood ran cold.

"So you are more than some common brute. Come, step closer, bring your tail in from the cold."

He hesitated.

By now his eyes had adjusted to the candlelight, the small flames reflected in her metallic face.

It wasn't fear that made him pause. He mastered that emotion long ago. It was the unplaceable alienness in the way she moved, her sightless eyes continuously scanning the room.

Only a moment's hesitation, but enough for her to notice. She laughed again, quieter this time as he approached the table in the center of her hut. The hides in the doorway fell shut behind him.

Her voice hovered above a whisper. "Yes, I know what you are, too. I can smell your reptile blood from here."

Candle smoke swirled and danced through the air, obscuring her face as she sat across from him. He placed his hands flat on the table, dried blood still caked around his sharpened nails.

Her face stopped moving for a moment, tilting to the side like an animal. "It is you, isn't it? Yix. The one they scour the lands to find. Is it not so?"

His tongue flicked between his snout. The air tasted stale.

"The king has named you traitor. Was there not once an accord between you?"

He turned away from her accusing gaze and spit, "The king is a fool. I warned him the fungal hordes were on the move. Not until they were at his gates did he realize his mistake. Many paid for his arrogance with their lives."

His eyes closed.

"Including the one you love."

Zoh. The words burned as her image flashed behind his closed eyes. Her smile, her scent, her colorful sail. Her limp body, surrounded by the crushed remains of their unborn eggs.

He opened his eyes, both sets of lids sliding back.

"Her death was needless. His inaction killed her." Yix's tongue flicked in and out.

"Is that why the king says you burned down half of the kingdom? Slaughtered your own kind?" She smiled through the accusations.

"The fire cut off the enemy's advance. I did what needed to be done, severed the hand to save the arm. I only killed those who stood in my way."

"Did you enjoy killing your countrymen?" Her head scanned the slanted ceiling.

"Yes."

She nodded. "So now you are in need of a seer. And you come armed already with some knowledge of what I offer?"

He remained silent.

She nodded again and brought a small pot of water to the table. Her shriveled fingers reached into a pouch, pulling out a clump of some dried plant. She hummed quietly as the water burst into a boil, steam intermingling with smoke. Producing a cup, she deposited the plant material inside and poured the boiling water.

"What is it you seek?"

"I can't stay here. As you say, they're searching for me. I need a way forward."

"The temple?"

Yix nodded.

She leaned forward, her grin cutting through the steam and smoke, dead eyes looking directly into his. "Why there? I wonder if you know more than you let on? You shouldn't keep secrets from your seer, you know."

His tongue flicked the air. *A way forward.* He had chosen his words carefully.

She slid her face back into shadow. "Drink, betrayer."

He lifted the cup, downing its contents in one gulp. Yix's vision swam, colors bleeding together.

"Touch my hand. I will guide you."

He shuddered as he grabbed her outstretched hand, her metal skin cool against his scales. His body vibrated with a strange energy. The interior of the hut pulsed as if gasping for breath. The sensation nauseated him, and he closed his eyes.

Brightly colored shapes danced across his eyelids, moving in increasingly complex patterns in time with the pulsing.

"Hear my voice, traitorous one. Let your conscious mind move toward mine. I will show you what has been and what may yet be."

When Yix opened his eyes, he was hovering in the air. He looked down at himself seated at the table, his arm outstretched, his hand in the crone's. Though she still sat across the table, her voice whispered soft and intimate in his ear.

"What do you see?"

He spoke in a low murmur. "Us. Your hut. I'm floating above us."

"And when you look up?"

The night sky spread above him, the stars blazing bright and clear. The walls of the hut fell away, and he moved toward the sky.

"What do you see, brute?" Her voice cut through the fog of the drug.

"The stars."

"That is your way forward. Now look down. What do you see?"

He stood waist-deep in an ocean of blood, stretching to the horizon. The crimson liquid bubbled as charred bodies broke the surface around him. Bandits, occult warriors, fungal berserkers. Old foes long since vanquished. Friends fallen in battle. His beloved, Zoh, whose life he sought to restore at the temple.

"The dead." His voice wavered.

"They are the past, the way you have come. You must look ahead. Focus on what you seek."

He looked up from Zoh, his body rising from the ocean of blood as if guided by his gaze alone. Again the field of stars.

He turned as he ascended. The blood trailed him as if pouring from his body.

The corpses crested beneath him, a wave of the dead. He returned his gaze upwards and thought of his destination.

The temple. Not the Solar All-Father's seat of power, but the rumored true temple. Stars drifted past like leaves on a river. One particular star floated against the current. It grew larger as he approached. It was their sun, The Mother Egg, red and bloated. Sickly.

Their planet came into view—Grotta, the Nest. It swirled around the star in a wild orbit. The two celestial bodies changed size until they were equal, slowed until they sat next to each other. The drug was communicating with him. The crone had said the stars were his way forward.

The true temple was connected to the Mother Egg. How could he get there?

In response to his question, color drained from the two spheres, turning them white. He recoiled as they became the eyes of the crone, materializing before him. The drug shifted her face from its silvery metallic color to a mask of gold. The startle returned Yix to the hut, where the crone's hand no longer rested in his.

He opened one set of eyelids just as she was creeping a knife across the table, the blade smeared with pale blue liquid.

A rare poison.

He withdrew with a snarl, afterimages of his vision floating in the air like ghosts. She threw her hands up, screaming as the poisoned dagger fell to the floor.

His ax sliced through her outstretched arms and bit into her neck.

She had the consistency of rotten fruit—soupy flesh held together by sagging skin. Liquid metal flowed from her wounds, slow and viscous as an oozing sore. The tangy scent coated his nostrils. She laughed as he swung several heavy blows.

Decapitating her took a surprising amount of strength. Breathing heavily, he lifted her head. Bits of metal and wiring hung from her neck, smoking and popping. Her body dissolved into a shimmering puddle without the head to maintain its form.

She cackled, her head dangling from his grip by her thin hair. "You were meant to die, interloper! The future I showed you was the least probable outcome of events!" Her voice was thick with glee.

He raised her to eye level. The white emptiness continued to search. "And what was supposed to happen? You stick me with poison and deliver me, weak and shivering, to the king?"

She just smiled.

He lowered her head. "So much for that plan."

"You're a fool. You think this is my only body? I already summoned the king's best men and a new body. They shall have you within hours. And I will dance at your execution, filthy beast."

He considered this for a moment. The drug showed the Mother Egg and Grotta becoming her eyes in his vision.

"You're coming with me."

He rolled the satchel off his shoulder and loosened the drawstrings. The crone hissed as Yix shoved her head to the bottom of the tanned leather bag.

Yix climbed deep enough into the highlands to break the surface of the Smog Flats. When he looked back, endless gray clouds blanketed his homeland. Nothing remained for him there.

Afternoon became night as he pressed up the mountain. Exhaustion eventually caught him, and he slept huddled beneath a small outcropping. Between the wailing of the wind and the moans of the seer, he couldn't tell which chilled him more.

He dreamt of Zoh, her crumpled body on the floor of their hut. He stepped through the door again and again, the sight of her a shock every time.

An hour before dawn, he packed his bedroll, slinging the crone's head over his shoulder. The sky lightened as he traveled, and the ground leveled. The temple first appeared as an outline against the rising sun, the large dome silhouetted like an eclipse.

The wind carried the chanting of the monks, their voices rising in intensity as the sun crawled toward the sky. Rough stairs carved into the mountain lead him toward the temple.

Yix soon walked between the rows of monks as they bowed, over and over, to the rising sun. Their chants reached a fever pitch as the fiery disc cleared the dome. Their adulation sickened him, like maggots crawling across rotten meat. They were empty vessels, oblivious to his presence.

Leaving the rapt monks, he climbed more steps to the entrance. White columns lined the temple's front. His fingers brushed them as he passed, revealing a strange and uneven texture. Stopping to examine one, he found they were made of teeth. Millions of partially melted teeth formed each column.

He stepped inside the main chamber. The four walls were open, morning sunlight streaming in opposite where he stood.

The floor had the same uneven texture as the columns. Bone. An occasional skull gazed upwards, the empty grin devoid of teeth. The room was circular, with a high domed ceiling that had a large hole open to the sky in the center. On the ground beneath the hole was a circle, pale green along the outer edge. The interior of the circle was metal, glowing a faint electric blue.

Interrupting the stream of sunlight opposite him was a throne on a tall pedestal, and a staircase spiraling around the exterior. The Solar All-Father sat at the top, the shape of his golden ceremonial mask like one of the skulls staring up from the floor. Sunlight broke around him, a stone in the current. Yix stared at the mask, remembering the crone's golden face during his hallucination.

The All-Father's voice boomed in the silence of the temple. "This is a place of light. It will not hold one of the darkness such as you."

Yix stepped closer to the circle, sunlight reflecting off the blade of his ax.

"You bring a weapon here? Do you intend violence?" the All-Father asked. "Do you only interact with the world through violence?" His voice was lilting, mocking.

"I only wish to gain access to the temple, holy man. I will fight if I have to." He stood at the edge of the circle.

The All-Father stared down from the top of the throne. The faint blue glow from the center circle reflected off the mask. "You are in the temple."

He met the All-Father's stare, the ghost of a smile in the corner of his snout. "You know what I mean. The true temple."

The All-Father straightened up on the throne, and Yix knew that then the rumors were true.

"I see," the priest said before standing to his full height. His red ceremonial robes flowed past his feet, obscuring his body. They streamed behind him as he descended the spiraling stairs, sunlight giving them the appearance of blood pouring from his body. Another piece of Yix's vision come to life.

"Of course, you must know I am unable to grant you access to the true temple. Not on my own." The All-Father rounded the pedestal, off the steps and onto the floor.

Yix let his bag slide down his shoulder, reaching inside. The satchel fell away, leaving only the crone's head dangling in his grip. The All-Father gasped, confirming Yix was right to bring the head.

Their sun and planet had transformed into the eyes of the crone in his vision. She was the key. Her head rotated slowly, the rag bulging against her mouth.

Something flashed in the corner of Yix's vision. Before he could react, a knife dug itself into his hand. He dropped the head as pain exploded along his arm. The crone rolled away, skirting the edge of the circle.

He turned as the entrance filled with the king's men, their blades reflecting the sun like the All-Father's mask.

His eyes flicked across them. Five, the holy number of children born from the Mother Egg. They would be the king's five fastest warriors. He recognized their faces but not their names.

The king stood behind them with the crone's new body. "It's over. Surrender and I will show you the king's mercy—a quick death."

"You'd enjoy that, wouldn't you? You, who I once considered a brother."

"Even brothers can betray their kingdom," the king sneered.

"You call it a betrayal. You were never able to do what needed to be done. Never able to make the hard decisions."

Yix backed up as they advanced, closer to the All-Father.

"And look what those hard decisions cost you." The king spoke softly, his twisted face revealing that any lingering love between them was now dead.

"You speak to me of cost? I sacrificed for our people! I have *nothing* while you hold on to everything, even as the kingdom burns. You've always been weak!"

Yix closed one set of eyelids and let his pulse slow, the familiar calm before the storm of violence. Five warriors, the king, and the headless body of the crone. The All-Father and the witch's head. The room unfolded in his mind, a mental map of action.

He opened his eyes and threw his ax at the All-Father, who let out a surprised "Oh!" as the blade bit into his chest. Yix was already charging the lizard on the far left.

The warrior swung his sword too high. Yix ducked and lunged with his momentum, biting into exposed belly. The king's men were lightly armored, for quicker travel, and Yix's teeth easily tore into the lizard's guts. He ripped his head back, spilling them on the temple floor.

The next closest warrior thrust with his sword as the other three ran toward them to close the gap. Yix pulled the knife from his hand, using it to parry the blow. He swung around, his tail sweeping the warrior off his feet as Yix slashed his neck with the knife.

Yix faced the king and his three remaining lizards, who pointed swords at him like an accusation. He still held the knife, blood from his hand running hot down the length of his arm. The two warriors on either end of the trio circled him slowly, the one in the center pressing forward to pin him.

Yix let himself be led toward the warrior on his left, who moved to flank him with an open-jawed lunge. Yix pivoted, the jaws snapping on air. He drove the knife through the warrior's closed snout, his eyes widening in surprise as he fell to the ground.

The silhouette of the king signaled to the two remaining warriors, and Yix turned to face them. To his surprise, only one remained. The other ran toward where the crone's head had rolled across the floor.

Yix charged the warrior before him, knocking him off balance. The prone warrior managed a slash across Yix's side, his midsection flaring with pain. He reached his ax, lifting it from the chest of the All-Father as the lizard gurgled weakly on the floor.

The warrior near the crone's head lifted her, pulling the rag from her mouth.

"Behind you, you fool!" she shouted as Yix's ax cut through the warrior's neck. His body fell to the ground, limp. Yix grabbed the head, wrapping the hair around his fingers. She dangled from his grip, thrashing as she gnashed her teeth.

The final warrior stood between him and the king. Yix and the warrior circled each other slowly.

The warrior lunged.

Yix lurched backward, his tail holding his weight. The blade sliced the air inches from him.

He brought his ax down, a reverberating clang as the warrior blocked with his sword. Yix pressed his weight into the ax handle, forcing the warrior to push with his sword.

Yix swung the crone's head into his as hard as he could. The warrior took a stunned step back, his block weakening.

Yix swept the sword from the warrior's grip and it clattered to the floor. He swung his ax, digging the weapon into the warrior's abdomen. The lizard fell to one knee before the ax split his skull. The last warrior fell over, dead.

Yix was soaked in blood—his own and the dead's. He looked at the king and smiled between heaving breaths. "Whatever you hoped to accomplish has failed, your majesty."

The king stood still.

Their eyes met briefly as he looked past Yix. He followed the king's gaze and could just make out the path a half-mile below. A large host of warriors rode up the mountainside on iguanodon mounts.

They wouldn't take long to cross the distance.

He snarled at the king before diving to the dying body of the All-Father. Ripping the golden mask off, he put it on and stepped into the glowing metal circle.

The crone's head was still in his grip, and together with the All-Father's mask the true temple was unlocked. Bright light from the metal circle shot through the open ceiling, the inside of the mask providing separate illumination.

The crone's mouth opened to scream, but he couldn't hear it over the buzzing in his ears.

He closed his eyes against the intense light, but it bled through with faint blue undertones. His scales tingled as the air crackled, and he lifted off the ground.

The king and the body of the crone levitated beside him. He kicked the king toward the edge of the circle, almost knocking him free of the light.

They all shot through the open roof of the temple. Below them, the horde of riders crashed into the temple like a wave upon a cliffside.

They ascended rapidly within the pillar of light. From this elevation the whole of the mountain was visible. He traced his path through the highlands, back to the vast cloud covering the entirety of the Smog Flats. Beyond the mountains lay the Adjura Desert and the sparkling emerald waters of the Green Sea.

Still they climbed higher. He looked up and gasped. Thousands upon thousands of stars spread before him like seeds in the wind during the growing season. He approached the Mother Egg's other massive children, colorful siblings of his own world.

Drood, the Wanderer, its purple surface even more vibrant this close.

Rejna, the Sister. Old stories told of ancient lizardkin shooting themselves into the sky to live on Rejna's bright green surface. Even now lights dotted the surface, possible settlements.

Sharn, the Gravestone. Sharn rising at the beginning of the dry season was an ominous thing, a sure portent of death. They passed without incident, its dark brown surface brooding below them.

At last, The Mother Egg.

He could see nothing beyond the red boiling surface, ropey tendrils licking the emptiness of space. The brightness was too much to bear, his eyes straining. The light they traveled on paled in comparison.

With its full immensity before him, he understood why the sun cults worshiped it. He experienced a shrinking sensation as his mind recontextualized itself, and he surrendered to awe.

He moved toward a large object floating in orbit, a white metallic tube curved into a circle with no beginning or end.

The temple.

The vision in the hag's hut was now clear. It was the true temple, the secret the All-Father kept for himself. Yix wondered, had he ever dared to travel here?

The temple loomed over him, caught in its orbit like a microcosm of the solar system. As they approached they slowed. An opening appeared and they descended to the ground inside. The blue light disappeared. They had arrived.

No longer distracted by the wonders of the solar system, he remembered his fellow passengers. The king lay at his feet, his tail and one of his legs frozen.

He wasn't entirely within the blue light.

The king of the lizardkin had been exposed to hard vacuum for the duration of the trip. He lay shivering on the ground.

Yix shook his head. "You are a fool. There was a time when you were not, but now it is all you are."

The king looked up.

"You are not worth the time it would take for me to kill you." Yix walked past him, the king grabbing at him as he did.

The crone's spare body was gone, but her head remained in his hand. Her mouth moved with no sound, perhaps affected by their method of travel. He threw it to the ground.

"Goodbye, seer." He stomped his foot down. The head imploded with a crunch. Its remains liquefied and pooled together, like her body.

He continued on and walked through the temple, observing the strange, clean curves of his surroundings. Low lighting revealed occasional windows to the starry blackness of space.

He stumbled and remembered that he was still bleeding, trailing red behind him like a slug. Yix placed a hand on his abdominal wound and applied firm pressure. He leaned against the wall as he walked, his ax serving as a crutch.

The corridor had many closed metal doors with no handles, no visible way to open them. Eventually, the corridor opened into a larger room with a glass ceiling. The sun burned beyond the glass, light invading every corner. He took his hand off of his wound to shield his eyes until they adjusted. A small altar was positioned to face the star.

He approached and a three-dimensional representation of the sun hovered above the altar. The small dot of the temple's orbit suggested the image existed in real-time. The image zoomed out, and one by one the planets came into view. First the Gravestone, then the Sister, the Wanderer. His own world, Grotta, the Nest. Finally Chin, the Father.

He fell to his knees, both exhaustion and reverence. The image zoomed in on the sun, the image of the crimson egg a crude imitation of the enormity outside.

He'd never been religious, but now, at the end of all things, what was left? Kneeling in the true temple, journeying through the void to the indescribably vast orb, how could he deny it?

"Mother Egg, creator and giver of life, hear my prayers. Please give me back my love Zoh, the light of my life, all that truly mattered, and you can take me into your shell for whatever purpose you see fit." He bowed and continued to bleed.

The miniature sun glowed intensely, the image filling the room before shrinking back to a small shimmering ball. His body tingled as the tide of light moved past him.

He spun around at footsteps in the corridor, expecting the king to come through the door. Instead, Zoh, restored and radiant, stood before him. His breath caught in his throat.

"My love, you are dying." Her voice sounded lovely and melodious. His eyes filled with tears at the hope that this wasn't some trick of his dying brain.

"Did it work? Are you real?"

He tried to stand but his legs could no longer hold his weight. Zoh rushed over to him, kneeling and putting a hand on his cheek.

"The temple recreated me from your memories, my love." She stroked the top of his head.

"I don't understand..." he said, coughing.

"It doesn't matter, my sweet Yix. I'm waiting for you, inside the shell of the Mother Egg. Come be with me, be with our children."

He smiled. "I'm so happy not to die alone."

"You'll never be alone again."

Zoh smiled at him, the sun reflecting off her scales. It filled her pupils, her eyes glowing with their own small stars.

The floor of the temple bulged downwards, forming a bubble with clear walls around them. The bubble broke free from the temple, drifting toward the massive burning ball of gas.

Yix held Zoh tight as the temperature soared, his life spilling from his wound.

The bubble sank into the shell of the Mother Egg and was gone.

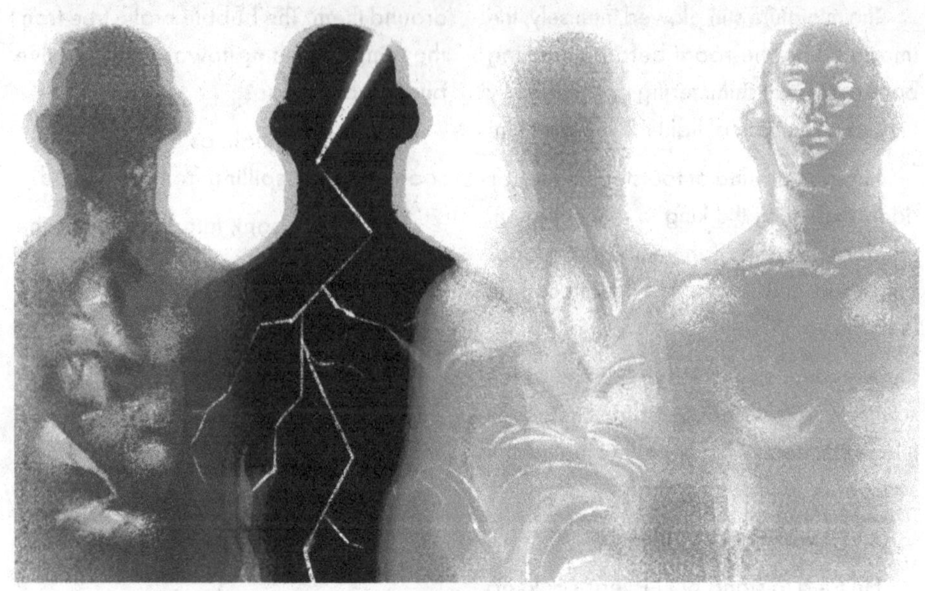

KIERAN O'MANT

BEING EMILY WAS TOO HARD

My name is Thim. I live in Habitat 32.

'Thim' is a word that I invented. It is a noun. It means nothing. I chose it to be my name because I don't think of myself as being any particular thing, and I definitely don't think of myself as being any particular thing that I have a word for.

There are a lot of words that don't mean a particular thing, as far as I know.

There are words that mean things that don't exist anymore, or words that refer to things that could never possibly exist. There are also words that refer to things that I cannot see.

I was going to call myself *'Convection'* or *'Sibilance.'* But I couldn't. These things have context, somewhere, even if they don't have any context to me.

I remember before I was called Thim.

I called myself *'Hello'* for a while, because that is how the computers greeted me. I then called myself *'Operator,'* because that is what they called me after "hello" — and I learned that "hello" is a salutation.

'Operator' was at least a noun. But it already meant something, and what it meant was not something that I at all connected to myself.

I'm not the first, and I'm not the last. There have been lots here. Outside there is a lot of red rock, inside a lot of metal and a lot of plants. These are more nouns, and therefore refer to a single, definite thing. Nouns aren't about context. That is why a noun can be a name.

I used to think I knew a great many things, because I knew everything about the world around me. This was before I named myself. This is when I was 'Operator.' Now I am not sure how much I know. I know this language—something I never thought of until recently. I think I'm the only one that uses it, though, so I don't know if that makes it an important thing to know.

I'm going to tell you about the others who lived here. They have a lot of things to say, but it's all in a lot of places. I think they wanted it to reach someone. It might even be me. I have been thinking that I will collect everything they say and store it in one place. I've chosen what I think are the important parts.

The first person to live here was called 'Emily.' Emily is a noun, as well.

✧

My name is Emily.
The Habitats should remain funct-ioning and solid indefinitely.

We did... incredible work on them. I never thought we'd have to test them like this. None of us ever thought it would be necessary, why did we ever install all of this? It must have taken so much time. So much money.

So many of them—everywhere, scattered—all I can think about is that I once wanted to call them "Terrariums." I said that "Habitat" sounded stupid. Terrarium would have been more fitting; terrariums can be sealed, they contain plants, terrariums contain unique environments. This is a very, very *singular* environment.

✧

It's very dark out. I don't know if there'll be much to look at when the dark clears.

I don't think there will. I don't... I really don't think so.

[Is transmission finished?]

No. No, wait. Give me a minute. I just. Give me a minute.

[Is transmission finished?]

No.

[Is transmission finished?]

No.

[Is transmission finished?]

[Transmission timed out]

✧

I thought I saw a light out there. I think it's been getting lighter over-all, but I can't really...

I saw a light out there, though. It was bright and red and angry. It reminded me of lightning, but it was the wrong colour.

William, I'm so sorry.

I've decided I'm not going through this anymore.

I thought about suicide. It seems irresponsible. There are a lot of habitats out there, and there are options now. We could [unable to parse] very long distances, but the conditions weren't perfect, no real guarantee... I mean, what is a mind? That's what some said. Surely if we just piece it straight back together...

There were possibilities, of course. By taking it apart, we could put it back together different. Completely reborn. Some were very excited about this—I mean, we all were, but many people, the body they were in was wrong and this was a way out of that. For a while we were so excited about the work we could do from there, but then William and me...

I've already explained what we did. There isn't anything left. William's still out there, somewhere. I dream about him. I'm very scared of him.

I'm not going to be Emily anymore.

I'm going to take myself apart—it's as good as death, some said. Maybe it is, maybe it isn't. I don't know. I never knew, none of us did. That's why it was hardly used—barely at all.

But I can go to another Habitat, be put back together there. Either me or somebody else. Just as long as there's somebody.

The first person after Emily was very different.

He was a lot like me—he got into the files, read them. He learned a lot. He listened to everything Emily had to say—he cared about her a very, very great deal. There isn't much to record from him. He just listened to her recordings, then recorded his own discussing how they made him feel, then listened again, then recorded again. He did this for a very long time.

It took me a long time to realise that the second person, who called himself William, and Emily happened in this order. They talk about, and to, each other, but eventually the computers explained to me that Emily came first. She was talking to somebody different, who is also called William, but who I don't think was with her. The computer says she was alone, like the rest of us, but the computer doesn't always seem to know everything. I think it can become confused, or it can't see into certain places. A lot of the people talk about someone else, even though the

BEING EMILY WAS TOO HARD

computer says they're alone. There's *'The Last Match'* or *'Burning Man'* or just one called *'Fire,'* which is a noun that is used for something else and it upsets me that it is used as a name. A lot of them are just descriptions.

There was just a flash outside. It was red, like a very sudden sunrise. It's not something I've seen before, but it isn't really surprising. Lots of new things have happened since I've been here, especially with the sky and with light.

Emily said that the sky was changing.

I've just found a transcript. Now I can read as well as hear Emily's words every night—is this wrong? It's hard to explain, but it does feel somehow wrong. Perhaps I'm not meant to be able to second-guess her? Perhaps her words, spoken aloud, should be enough for me? Or perhaps it's just that her voice isn't a part of these. Her voice is so vital—so important. I need that voice. Taking her voice out of her words seems almost... blasphemous. Words are for teaching, explaining, understanding. But voice is something else—voice is for contact, for connection, for exaltation.

I don't think I will read the transcripts. I think I will be content with her voice.

The latest transcript mentions William again. I'm starting to wonder about this other man. I can't remember too clearly where I got my name from, but I can't help but feel that this other William must have something to do with it. Was it some piece of Emily's guidance that led me to this name? Who was—or is—this other man? I feel a kind of envy for him. Am I just a homage to him? Did Emily feel something for this person that she should name her greatest gift after him?

I, alone, have life now. Whoever this man is or was, *I* am what is important now. It is my name alone.

The latest recording was illuminating. I feel I am approaching a truer kind of clarity with the books to guide my mind, and Emily's voice to guide my soul. Questions arise daily, but the answers are so obvious so long as I have her. Her voice, the words she speaks, give me context and clarity. I cannot imagine life without her.

Today's recording carried instructions on how to better use Emily's gifts. I've been asking the machines—they understand a specific language, only certain words. Emily has given me those words, and now they must provide me with answers. Her mastery over them is a miracle to see, and now that miracle is mine as well.

There have been flashes of red these past few days, just as Emily's words become their most revelatory. Is it a sign? Today, I am going to break my one rule. Emily has promised a great Explanation in her next recording.

Although I have already listened to one today, I will listen to another. I am nearing the end, it is true, but once I reach it, I will listen to them all again. When I first heard them I was so ignorant—what new secrets will I be able to parse from them?

✧

The computer says that William wasn't around very long, but that he was very busy most days.

I'm also very busy most days, but not in the same way. I haven't read the books, because they are not as important or as interesting as what the computer has to say. The books are about the past, or things that don't exist, or things that might exist but that don't do anything at the moment. The books can tell me things, but the things might not be true, and if I learn about the computer then I can change what is around me. The computer *is* change.

And Emily never wrote a book, and Emily made this place. I want to hear what Emily has to say, and I want to learn what Emily learned. William liked talking about Emily, but he could never do what she did. I can. And that's what I'm going to do.

Emily, William and several others all made somebody else. I don't know who made me, but Emily made William and then William made someone else. Emily and William both did something that made them... stop. When they made somebody new, they didn't leave themselves behind. They were used up, like how fire eats wood. I'm not going to do that.

I've found out how to make somebody new, and I won't need to be taken apart to build them. Emily didn't seem to be scared to die, but there was a lot wrong with Emily, I think. She was very scared of other things, perhaps so scared, that that was why she wasn't scared to die. I'm scared to die—nobody seems to know what happens after it, and everybody was so careful not to die, and all the computers are trying very hard not to let it happen to me. I trust the computers. I understand them, and I don't understand death.

I've got information from where Emily used to be. I'm going to rebuild her.

I'm going to place her in Habitat 33, which is a "Full Functionality Habitat," and I'm going to let her grow up. The computers are going to look after her, and I'm going to talk to her every day. I'm going to ask her a lot of questions. I want to understand a lot of things, like what things are and aren't true, and what happened to the world and how, and why she wasn't scared of death and who William was. I'm going to do it now.

Computer, shut the grates please. The red flashes are upsetting me.

"Your name is Emily." These were the first words ever said to me. I don't know how I knew what they meant, but I did.

I was told that I was in Habitat 33, and that this was where I would

BEING EMILY WAS TOO HARD

live and die. The voice was strange. I'll still never know if it was because it was the first voice I ever heard, or because of something else entirely. I have not had the opportunity for comparison, and it seems unlikely I ever will if all that I've heard is correct.

I've heard the voices of the machines many times; they've become more familiar to me even than my own. But that original voice—the one that first spoke to me—I hear no more. It told me things. Basic, simple things—the foundations of my life.

Then it was silent. For twenty-two years.

✧

I've read the books, where I can. I've listened to the recordings. I've studied the maps.

It comes easily to me, questions of philosophy and technology arrive already half-answered. I have no basis for comparison.

Is it this easy for everyone?

I know that it is not. I know it is not this easy strongly enough that, even in my isolation, I recognise it as notable. It reminds me very much of the process of forgetting your dreams, but in reverse. I start with one feature, which sharpens until other features form around it.

Eventually, these create a structure—a shape of a thought, and then I understand.

If I am alone, why do I know that I am special?

If I'm alone, who taught me that there was anything else to be compared to? If I am alone, then *how* do I understand that I *am* alone?

✧

I feel guilt at the way things are. It is distant, almost too far to feel, but it is there. It's like regretting your own actions as a child: though you know you could not reasonably be held accountable, you still understand that they were wrong. It's unfair to expect more from yourself, and yet you still think you should have been *better*.

I've read the logs. I've heard the voices. I know what somebody else did, but is that me? Are any of them me? If this is all I've ever known, why am I still dissatisfied with the cold, recorded voices echoing at me over the decades? Is this the yearning of early man for the heavens? Or is it the yearning of an exile for a nearly-forgotten home country? Is there any point identifying the distinction? Is there any point in borrowing these comparisons, these analogies, from the history of a dead world?

Habit 33 is exceptional. It was a hub. The computer told me this, but I already suspected. I wonder at the power here—could I disseminate myself, as did all my predecessors? I'm sure I could.

Will I?

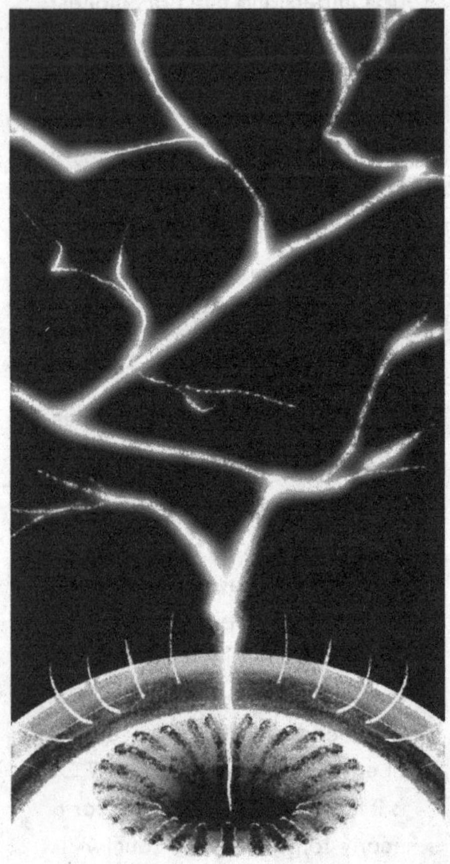

I don't understand the compulsion they felt any more than I understand who they were, but there... there is a precedent, isn't there?

When every single one before me has done so, is it foolish to spurn their example? Or is it more foolish to follow their design without comprehension?

Life is difficult, being me is terrifying, it is hard.

Why is it hard?

I look back at the old habitats. There is no way to trace the recordings anymore, but I suspect that many of the ones that have since stopped responding are the ones that these others inhabited.

What happened to them? Why do they all talk about a burning man, or a fire of some kind? Why do they all see the red lights, and why do they all say that the sky is changing? Is this metaphor, or allusion? Do they simply not understand what they're actually seeing?

The most recent to go dark was Habitat 32.

What happened to it?

I've just seen a red flash of light. I'm scared.

William, I'm so sorry.

BEING EMILY WAS TOO HARD

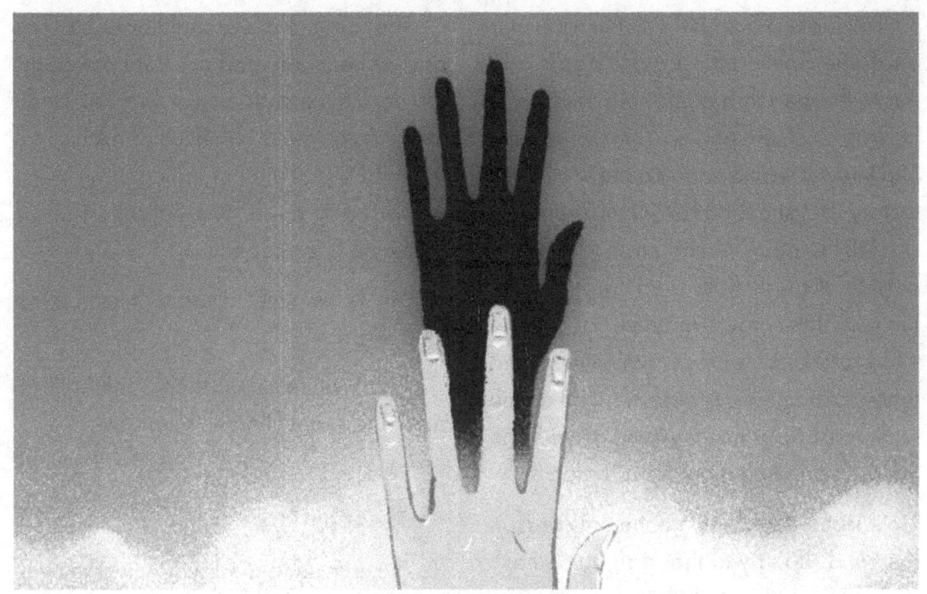

LEO VLADIMIRSKY

A COLLECTION OF ENDINGS

"...kicking off of the huge concrete blocks of the pylons. It's *Woman and Voat* vs. *Bridge* at this point. The tide is surging and..." Lily felt a gentle tickle on her right forearm.

She looked away from Amy, who was waving her arms and talking in the middle of the living room. The fly's ski-goggle iridescent eyes picked up the motionless candle flames, its body a jungle of greens. Then it bit her.

"Motherfucker!"

Seven heads, tanned and lined as only sailors' get, snapped around to look at her.

"Sorry Amy," Lily said. "Greenhead got me." She lifted her arm to show the small drop of blood now pooling on her skin.

"The wind won't save us from the biting flies anymore," Amy said and chuckled. "Gotta keep your skin covered."

"Here," Stephen said, tossing Lily a blanket. "It'll do for now."

"Thanks." She wrapped it around herself.

"Where was I?" Amy said.

"You were under the Tappan Zee Bridge."

Amy snapped her fingers. "Right. So this Tyler Craft was twin-keeled, and not built..."

Lily looked across the living room, through the open sliding glass doors and out to the beach beyond. No wind, and no waves. Inside and out, the air was still. She knew it would soon be her turn to tell a story, but she didn't want to. Even now she felt the dead ocean urging her to go outside. A bright flash from the TV caught her eye. The screen, mounted above the white-bricked fireplace, was muted and tuned to the news. A reporter walked the tarmac at Spaceport America with the Southwest evacuation coordinator.

"...sturdy flip-flops are the only reason the wind didn't win that day and smash me and the Nikita to bits," Amy said, raising her highball. "To the dying wind!"

Everyone raised their glasses, "To the dying wind!" They drank.

Amy flopped back down on the Papasan chair, legs hanging over one side

"I'll be damned if I'm ever getting up again," she said.

"Nice story," said Andy, drying his beard with the back of his hand. "Though why you were wearing flip-flops sailing solo up the Hudson is beyond me. That's a brutal river."

Amy threw him a dirty look over the edge of her rum and tonic. "Next thing you'll tell me I should have had my life jacket on too."

"Safety first," he said, and laughed. "Alright. Looks like the only person left is Lily. Get on the stump!"

The room clapped and hooted. Every part of her screamed *no*. But how could she deny her friends an elegy for the wind? Even Max, who'd gotten so drunk he started sobbing at the beginning of his story, managed to finish. She lifted herself off the white linen cube.

"You know guys," Lily said. "I need some air."

"Get it while it's still there, right?" Amy said. The room filled with laughter.

"No!"

"Too soon!"

The comments died suddenly. The overwhelming stillness outside came crashing in through the dark, bringing an awful silence.

"You owe us your story when you get back," said Andy. "No walking into the ocean."

Lily put her hand on her heart.

"You have my word. Can't promise a happy ending though."

With a sure-footed walk, perfected on decades of slippery decks, she headed toward the open doors, weaving around shabby-chic couches, worn rugs, and sleeping dogs.

"Lily! Take my jacket. You'll get eaten alive." She paused for a moment in the open doorway and caught the nylon windbreaker that Amy tossed to her.

The conversation quickly resumed and the clatter of ice and rum filled the air behind her.

    A COLLECTION OF ENDINGS

Lily turned and stared out at the darkness before stepping across the threshold. Her bare feet picked up no grit as she crossed the clean patio, and the cold sand was a shock when she reached the beach. Under the bright moon, she could see up and down the coast for miles. With no wind to scour them away, uncountable footprints cratered the shore. The night sky was frozen in the sea, and it gave her the uneasy feeling of floating in space. An even row of dried kelp and egg cases marked the high tide line. She jumped into the still water, expecting it to be cold, But it wasn't. Air, sand, and sea were stasis.

She felt bad breaking the calm, so she walked back to the tide line and followed it, staying on the wet side. She'd never heard the sea so quiet. The game they were playing back in the house, airing their mock hatred for the dying wind, made perfect sense. Sailors were always subservient to the wind. But, even now, she couldn't pretend that she hated it. Without it, the sea would be just like space: cold, dead, and bright.

The few neighboring houses were dark, but down the shore stood a bright forest of colored pinpoints. The sailors at the marina were blazing every light on their boats in protest. She desperately wanted to hear the sound of lanyards clanking on masts, of whipping flags and wheezing fenders and tolling bells. But those sounds were gone forever. She turned her back on the city of lights, sat down in the sand and cried. The pull to get up and walk into that nothing, until her own body cooled and joined the rest of the dying planet, was overwhelming. Her tears smeared the cacophony of motionless stars on the water. After a while, she had to turn away from the sea.

"Nice night. All things considered."

Lily looked up with a glare at a middle-aged man in boat shoes and a worn pink polo. His hair was short and his beard full and blonde. A fellow sailor.

"What's nice about it?"

"Sorry to bother you," he said, and began to walk on.

"No, it's ok," Lily said. "I'm just..."

The man nodded. "I understand. Mind if I sit?"

"I'll make room," she said, sliding over a foot on the desolate beach.

He laughed and eased himself down into the cold sand. Lily thought he looked very familiar.

"Don't you skipper that J-30? What was it called... Pale Rider? Easy Rider?"

"No," he said. "I don't sail around here."

She shook her head.

"Too bad. I love J-Boats. Learned to race on one of those. They could sail on a sneeze. I guess this is the end of all that. And of us."

He shrugged

"I've seen a lot of endings," he said. "This one is pretty peaceful."

"What?"

"Take the K/T extinction, for example. You've never seen fire like that."

She frowned.

"The thing that killed the dinosaurs?"

"Them and everything else that weighed more than a couple of pounds," he said. "Although without it, humanity wouldn't be here."

"I guess not."

"Do you want to see?"

"Are you trying to invite me back to your beach house or something?" she asked. "I'm pretty sure that's the kind of shit people warn you against."

He laughed. "No, I can show you here."

"I'm not sure I—"

But his hand was on Lily's shoulder before she could finish.

Then... standing on a beach under a bright, hot sun. Strange trees, like distant tropical cousins to the pines and ferns she had grown up with on the coast of Maine, crowded the edge of the narrow strip of sand. She opened her mouth to breathe and the wind, thick and rich, poured in over her lips and down her throat into her lungs.

"What is..."

The man was looking into the sky.

"There," he said, pointing.

A dark object was growing at an incredible speed.

"Just watch. This is the ending."

The object grew and grew, until Lily could make out ridges and craters pitting its surface. Soon it blocked the sun, and the beach was dark. All she heard was the buzzing of foreign insects. Her hair blew in the rushing wind. Then the air caught on fire.

He pulled his hand back from her. They were back on the pock-marked beach, sitting in the same place above the high tide line.

"See what I mean?" he said.

Lily tried jumping to her feet, but stumbled and scrambled backwards. The man brushed his hair roughly.

"It's so weird not having sand in my hair after spending the day at the beach. No wind to blow it around, I guess."

Lily stared at him, mid-crouch.

"What was that?"

He picked up a small pebble, smoothed by countless lost waves.

"That was the K-T meteor. Well, asteroid I guess. You'd think after having seen as many of them as I have that I'd get it right by now."

He chuckled and tossed the pebble into the water.

"Who the fuck are you?" said Lily.

"I collect endings," he said.

"What the hell does that mean?"

"You know what they say about trees falling in forests?"

She sank back down in the sand.

"You always see that scene with the dinosaurs looking over their shoulders," she said. "I figured that they'd heard it or something, but it was so quiet."

"It's not always the way that it looks in movies."

She stared out at the dead water and stars and moonlight.

"Well, Mr. Collector," she said. "What else you got?"

In the moonlight she could see him smile as he stretched out his arm.

✧

... *cracks of gunfire and red mist surround the head of the man in the back seat of the convertible.*

... *metallic ping of pellets falling down a pipe and the shower room smells like almonds.*

... *its pale body, enormous, settles in a slow-motion puff on the ocean floor.*

"... sabachthani!" he shouts, and his body slumps, hanging in an unnatural position from the nails in his hands and feet.

... *last note rings out and the audience is silent.*

... *closes her beak and listens for a reply in the cool dark forest.*

... *ring rolls a little on the coffee table then stops.*

... *totally unlike the pirogues she's used to, coming closer and closer.*

... *the stubble visible on his arm, as he locks the cockpit door.*

... *cries out as she comes.*

... *on top of a coffin, bobbing gently in the water.*

... *as the last star in the sky disappears.*

✧

His hand paused just by her right ear, before he pulled it back.

Lily buried her hands and feet in the soft cool sand. "You're here to capture the last breath of wind."

He rocked his head, subtly, side-to-side.

"I am here to collect an ending," he said. "Which ending is entirely up to me."

She felt that pull again towards the water and burrowed her feet deeper into the sand, trying to hold on.

"I guess I don't believe it... that the wind is really going to stop blowing," she said. "That the oceans will die. They're my life. They're all of our lives. The earth is ocean. How can it just end?"

A small ghost-crab scuttled over her toes.

"Everything ends."

She pulled her hands out of the sand and began to smooth the area around her. The contrast between the featureless square in front of her and the vast pitted beach filled her with sadness.

"Is that supposed to be comforting?"

He sighed.

"When I started collecting endings, I went for the big bangs."

Lily looked over at him, head cocked.

"Har har."

"Sorry," he said, chuckling. "I went for the dramatic. Explosions. Violence. Blood. The K-T, that was my first. No subtlety."

A small swarm of no-see-ums buzzed in her ears. She swatted them away. He raked the sand with his fingers, unearthing a near-perfect scallop shell.

"And now?"

"I realized that endings are not what I thought they were. They're the moment of change, when nothing can go back to the way it was. It's not the explosion, it's the decision to drop the bomb. And it doesn't have to be bad. It could just as easily be a book closing or an unfinished letter, a gun loading or rope being tied. Some endings even start with a beginning."

"So why aren't you a collector of beginnings, then?"

"There's only one beginning. Capital 'B' beginning, I mean," he said. "Besides... endings are a lot more interesting."

"Will you have an ending?" she asked.

He threw the shell sidearm into the sea. It skipped and each time it glanced off the water it left a single concentric ripple.

"No," he said. "I will not. I only have a beginning."

The waves from the shell passed through each other. He threw another one.

"Have you decided what this ending will be?"

"Not yet," he said. "But I have a good one in mind."

"I don't suppose you can tell me."

"I can't," he said. "I'm sorry."

She chuckled.

"Well, it was worth a shot," she said.

"I do have one more ending I want to show you," he said. "It might help you understand."

She took a deep breath and blew out hard. "Let's do it."

He reached out.

✧

... hands trying to clutch the murky blue water. With each pass, the water whitened with bubbles.

✧

He drew back his hand, smiling at her.

"That was me!" she said.

He nodded.

"We were on the shore at Mount Desert Island. My brother was supposed to watch me when my parents went for a walk, but he disappeared to talk to some girls and I decided to go into the ocean. My father heard my splashing and dove into the water, sandals, shorts and all, and pulled me out."

        A COLLECTION OF ENDINGS

"That's right."

"But I didn't die. If anything, that was the reason I learned to swim and to sail."

"Not all endings end in death," he said. "Now do you understand?"

Lily leaned back, away from the water.

"I think so."

"Good."

The waves from the shells had disappeared, and the sea was frozen again. She stared at it until her peripheral vision went dark and all she saw was stars. She looked over. His eyes were fixed on the horizon.

"It is beautiful," she said. "In its own way. I suppose people must see the ocean the way I see the sky."

He nodded.

"That is true."

"Maybe it won't be so bad to be up there."

"That ending is entirely up to you."

Lily stood up and brushed the sand from her pants. "I think I've got to get back to my friends," she said, and stuck out her hand.

"Thanks for the chat," he said, taking it and pulling himself up.

"Do you want to come join us?" she asked. "We're sitting around and telling sad stories of the death of kings. You'd be a real hit at this party."

He looked out towards the ocean, then back at her.

"We'll see," he said. "Maybe I'll join you later."

"Fair enough. See you around."

She headed towards the house, the bright lights in the living room her beacon. As she got closer, she realized her friends were silent. All eyes were on the television, now unmuted.

"... reports of no wind at all on the entire seaboard. We'll go live to our weatherperson Julia Markovic on the boardwalk in Coney Island in a moment, but first, here is the schedule for the first round of evacuation launches. Cape Canaveral..."

She pointed at the TV.

"Turn that fucking thing off," said Lily. "I believe it's my turn and I don't want you people distracted."

They turned to her. She took a deep breath.

"My story starts with an ending..."

PAUL C.K. SPEARS

BUREAUCRACY OF WEIRD: UFO MYTHS, DEBUNKED!

The study of unidentified flying objects has always been colored by pop culture. From the 1956 classic horror film *"Earth vs. The Flying Saucers,"* to more recent cultural juggernauts like *"Men in Black"* and Jordan Peele's *"Nope,"* Americans have long absorbed a diet of flying saucer entertainment. But what happens when this longstanding sci-fi tradition crosses over into reality? How can we reconcile the thrills and chills of fake UFOs when the same subject is now seriously discussed in the halls of government?

As we've covered previously, the United States government seems to have a sizeable interest in UFOs[1], recently rebranded in the media as "UAPs," or Unidentified Aerial Phenomenon. From the original UAP video leaks in 2019, to an official DNI intelligence report in June 2021 and a recent Congressional hearing[2], these objects are once again becoming difficult to ignore, as they were in the 1950s, and then again in the 1970s.

And understandably, most Americans aren't sure what to make of all this. Surely, the American government can't be serious about spending money on flying saucer research? And yet, the Pentagon has set up a whole new office—the All-Domain Anomaly Resolution Office[3]—to do exactly that.

What are we to make of all this?

When in doubt, we default back to what we know. And what Americans know better than anything else is our own pop culture. We all know the tropes of flying saucers in fiction—craft that are basically, conventional spacecraft, piloted by little creepy guys from Zeta Reticuli, coming to steal our cows or probe us. The problem is, such tropes contradict witness accounts of *actual* unknown craft, which can be a lot more serious and frightening than what we laughingly imagine them to be.

Now, with increased public and government interest in UAP reporting, it's time to clear up a few outdated myths.

While we all enjoy a good pop culture UFO, these inaccurate and lasting depictions of "little green men" and "death rays" only serve to muddle the waters of more serious UFO research. If we ever want to figure out what's happening in our skies,

---

1   *Scientific American, "Experts Weigh In on Pentagon UFO Report"*
2   *CNET Video, "Everything Revealed at the Congressional UFO Hearing in 10 Minutes"*
3   *Twitter, "Official Twitter account of the @deptofdefense's All-domain Anomaly Resolution Office."*

and apply scientific rigor, we have to stop referring back to Spielberg and Shyamalan-style aliens in our UFO assumptions. We have to learn the difference between facts, as far as we can currently parse them, and fiction. So let's review a few of the most popular UFO myths, and find out which ones match real eyewitness accounts—and which ones are too "out of this world" to be considered seriously.

[Note: since this article deals with 20th century pop culture, for the sake of clarity we'll refer to these objects as "UFOs" rather than the modern term, "UAP."]

✧

MYTH #1:

UFOS ARE ALL DISC-SHAPED FLYING SAUCERS

"UFOs" come in a dizzying variety of shapes, colors and behaviors. Occasionally, witnesses do report the "classic" flying saucer shape, as Guillermo Del Toro once did in an interview with Hollywood Reporter.[4] Some appear (at least on the surface) to be metallic flying craft, while others appear much less "nuts and bolts" in nature, and may display strange properties, composition, and behaviors. Hovering black triangles, silver cylinders, white "Tic Tac" shaped craft, and countless others have been reported.

Some of the wilder accounts describe eerie, shifting geometric shapes and even,

according to researcher George Knapp[5], "swirling balls of living light." Over the years, almost every imaginable UFO shape has been reported, from flying tube shaped "cigar" UFOs to weirder shapes like ovals, diamond-shaped craft, and even zeppelin-shaped objects.

✧

MYTH #2:

THE GOVERNMENT KNOWS EXACTLY WHAT UFOS ARE, AND THEY'VE BEEN HIDING THE TRUTH SINCE ROSWELL

There are some clues indicating the government *might* have UFO materials or a piece of one—interviews with the late Senator Harry Reid suggest that Reid requested to see such materials, and was denied. However there's no evidence the American government, has any *functional* UFO technologies, much less a functioning craft, in their possession. And this might be a good thing.

If any government had even a fraction of the technology displayed on leaked Navy UAP videos like the "GIMBAL" and "FLIR" footage, the world would be a very different place—because the technical capabilities of UFOs are what those in the defense industry call "next-generation" technology. Navy pilots such as Lieutenant Ryan Graves, who appeared on '60 Minutes' in 2021 to discuss UAPs, refers to them as a "serious security risk."

---

4   *Hollywood Reporter, "Guillermo del Toro on Seeing a UFO, Hearing Ghosts and Shaping 'Water'"*
5   *George Knapp, "Hunt for the Skinwalker"*

A recent NIH paper[6] suggests that UFOs have quite an array of abilities, including perfect flight in most weather conditions, lack of emissions, and a lack of heat signatures. Radio technician Kevin Day, who served on the *USS Princeton* in 2004, has discussed how UAPs have a "trans-medium" ability to go from the skies to underwater in mere seconds.[7]

If any country on Earth had these technologies in its possession, it could achieve complete air supremacy across the globe. Think about it—how would you even fight a craft that goes supersonic without breaking the sound barrier, intrudes on restricted airspace with complete impunity[8], and can jam military communications frequencies with ease—as UAPs have repeatedly been reported to do?

However, this doesn't mean the Pentagon knows nothing about UFOs—as we've seen previously, the Department of Defense is not eager to discuss the topic, and with good reason. Their inaction and obfuscation of the UFO issue has not aged well, making them look either incompetent in the face of the problem, or directly nefarious.

✧

MYTH #3:

THE GOVERNMENT SENDS IN "MEN IN BLACK" TO COVER UP UFO INCIDENTS/SIGHTINGS

This myth started with a man named Albert Bender, a high-strung horror nerd in the 1950s who claimed he was being stalked by eerie, suit-clad apparitions. An associate of his took the story and ran with it, publishing a book titled *"They Knew Too Much About Flying Saucers."*

Soon after, the myth entered public consciousness. Decades later, this spooky trend culminated with *"X-Files"* and the *"Men In Black"* franchise, searing the image of the suit-clad UFO investigator into the public imagination.

On its face this seems absurd—of all the ways to keep tabs on UFO witnesses, tailing them in a suit and tie for months seems like the worst possible way to do so. However, some witnesses to UFOs *have* attested to being observed or watched after their sightings, and several have reported "hitchhiker" phenomenon—unusual or eerie occurrences in the weeks and months after UFO sightings. One of these reports comes from Dan Akroyd, who claims to have been "observed" by strange individuals after attempting to make a show about UFOs[9], back in 2002.

Finally, there have been accounts of government employees investigating UFO sightings in the wake of the events, asking questions and removing evidence. No such investigations have ever been officially acknowledged by the DOD or the

---

6   National Library of Medicine, *"Estimating Flight Characteristics of Anomalous Unidentified Aerial Vehicles"*

7   Ryan Sprague, *"He's the Reason We Know about the 'Tic Tac' UFO"*

8   CBS News, *" UFOs regularly spotted in restricted U.S. airspace, report on the phenomena due next month"*

9   IMDb, *"Dan Akroyd Unplugged on UFOs"*

intelligence community, with the exception of "Project Blue Book,"[10] an Air Force intelligence-gathering project canceled in December of 1969.

UFOS ARE PILOTED BY "LITTLE GREEN MEN" OR GREY ALIENS, WHO ABDUCT HUMANS FOR REASONS UNKNOWN

This is where we range into the murkier elements of UFO myth. While the GIMBAL and FLIR videos and the eyewitness accounts confirm that modern UFOs are real, physical objects, the question of whether they have occupants—and what those occupants might want—is much harder to answer. Rumors of extraterrestrial biological entities, or "EBEs," occupying or piloting UFOs is a staple of UFO lore. The most famous report of this kind came from the Betty and Barney Hill incident of 1961, a terrifying account of abduction and experimentation.

Obviously, no "EBE" has ever been caught on film, or confirmed by military hardware or official reports, unlike the strange craft currently bedeviling the Pentagon. And so we are left with many, many confusing witness reports about EBEs, quite a few of which are obvious hoaxes. The most notable of these was "Alien Autopsy," a 1995 hoax filmed by indie entrepreneur Ray Santilli. Santilli kept the hoax's myth alive for years, until he was eventually exposed as a fraud by researchers.

Furthermore, many UFO witnesses who report EBEs do so under prompting from "true believer" psychiatrists or interviewers, who may have agendas of their own.

But the sheer amount of witness accounts does invite curiosity. These accounts vary wildly, as does the appearance behavior of the EBEs described. Classic "grey" aliens, mantis-like insect EBEs, and "tall blonde humanoid" entities have all been reported, and what's more troubling is that some of these reports—however absurd they sound—start to look weirdly consistent when lined up with one another. What this signifies isn't entirely clear.

Many EBE close encounters come across as eerie, bizarre or utterly nonsensical in nature, and there is a persistent phenomenon of sightings involving "high strangeness": Reports of EBEs walking through walls, reports of "stopped time" or utter silence, or a sense of nameless dread when EBEs are witnessed, continue to pile up as the years roll on.

Sometimes the entities seem to behave like automatons, or appear "mechanical" in appearance and movement. Sometimes they speak, sometimes they don't. Sometimes they confront people in the wilderness, as with the Flatwoods Monster incident of 1952,[11] other times, they land on schoolyards and attempt to communicate with

---

10 Wikipedia, "Project Blue Book"
11 History.com, "In 1952, the Flatwoods Monster Terrified 6 Kids, a Mom, a Dog—and the Nation"

children, as in the alleged "Ariel School Incident" of 1994[12]. These accounts are all over the map—and therefore, pretty much impossible to prove or disprove.

Frankly, it's impossible to say at this point whether UFOs are occupied, and if so, what might be lurking inside. The accounts are simply too sketchy and unreliable to form any sort of solid hypothesis.

✦

ALL PEOPLE WHO CLAIM THAT THEY HAVE BEEN CONTACTED OR ABDUCTED BY UFOS ARE CRAZY, LYING, OR BOTH

Continuing from the previous theme, it's hard to discuss UFOs without discussing hoaxes. Human beings lie, and will happily do so if they see a potential for fame or attention or money. So when a person claims they've been abducted by little bug-eyed monsters, our first instinct is skepticism, and rightly so.

Yet the "abduction" narrative returns again and again, across the decades, seeping into pop-culture and becoming the butt of jokes time after time. Where did the alien abduction trope come from? Let's start with the "lost time" phenomenon.

The concept of "time loss" is a frequent element of UFO witness accounts.[13] The most famous example, that of Betty and Barney Hill in 1961, was dramatized in the 1966 book "The Interrupted Journey." The "time loss" myth goes as follows: First, witnesses see a UFO, and then (they claim) they find themselves several miles away, or sitting in their car on the side of the road, or even at home eating dinner. Aside from being creepy, the "lost time" accounts create an obvious gap: where did those memories go? Tales of alien abduction have risen to fill this gap over the years, but the origins of these tales are mired in pseudoscience, disinformation, and fraud.

In 1987, an alleged abductee named Whitley Strieber published "Communion," a record of his supposed "flashbacks" of alien abduction. It didn't take long for this concept to hit the mainstream. Just a few years later, on "The X-Files," writers were already using hypnotic regression as a method to introduce aliens to the storyline[14].

This fictional depiction is fairly close to what actually happened when abductees were studied in the 1970s; alleged abduction victims who underwent hypnotic-regression therapy described alien ships, or small creatures, or experiments. But these accounts were deeply unreliable, simply due to the nature of hypnotism itself. Regressive hypnotherapy has shown itself capable of planting false memories.[15] In addition, people under the influence of hypnosis have a tendency to regurgitate

---

12   BBC.com, "The schoolkids who said they saw 'aliens'"
13   Unsolved Mysteries, "UFO Abduction: Missing Time"
14   Clip from The X-Files: Mulder's Hypnotic Regression Therapy [S01E04]
15   Julia Shaw and Stephen Porter, " Constructing Rich False Memories of Committing Crime"

the prompts or ideas they are fed while in their trance.

But most abduction stories do share one strange commonality: there is a strong *emotional* component to these tales. The emotional response varies wildly in tone, from terrifying and surreal to blissful and religious,[16] but there is always a powerful *feeling* associated with the reported event—whether it's fear, or delight, or even rage.

This spurs an obvious question—why would a visit by alien beings feel frightening to some, and strangely joyful to others? No matter which way you look at it, there's an inconsistency here, and it points towards these accounts being dubious at best. Jacques Vallee[17], a famous UFO researcher, summed it up succinctly: there is a "sociological element," he claimed, to EBE abduction accounts. What exactly the "sociological element" is, remains to be seen. Is alien abduction a form of mass hysteria? Is it a hallucination, brought on by sleep paralysis? Or is there something weirder going on? Without more evidence, it's nearly impossible to say.

And over the years, hypnotherapy has not exactly improved its reputation. While it does show promise in treating PTSD,[18] it remains a pseudoscience at best, especially when it comes to bringing back "repressed" events or memories. Overzealous public trust in the veracity of hypnotherapy once

jump-started a Satanic Panic, after all. In the 1970s, several fanciful (and clearly absurd) accounts of "repressed Satanic abuse" were published[19] and America was swept into a moral panic, with Christian groups insisting a Satanic cabal lurked around every corner. Unfortunately, several "abduction victims" were caught up in the hypnotism craze, and the resulting accounts created nothing but chaos and confusion among UFO research groups.

To this day, it is unclear whether these "repressed" memories are real events that happened to abductees, or simply artifacts of the imagination, spawned by overzealous prompting while the subjects were under the altered state of hypnosis.

UFOS ARE INFILTRATING THE EARTH WITH HYBRID ALIENS

This colorful conspiracy theory was first popularized by figures like Bob Lazar, a self-proclaimed "whistleblower" eager to spin tales of underground facilities and lizard-like aliens working with the government. Like tales of abduction in general, there is little hard evidence to go on here. Some alleged witnesses have described alien-human hybrids or children during regressive hypno-therapy sessions, but again, hypnotherapy is a dubious tool at

---

16   *The Gardner News*, " *Local Halloween lore: The Andreasson Affair*"
17   *Wired.com*, "*Jacques Vallée Still Doesn't Know What UFOs Are*"
18   *National Library of Medicine*, " *New uses of hypnosis in the treatment of posttraumatic stress disorder*"
19   *Vox.com*, " *Why are we so worried about Satan?*"

best. Until we learn more about EBEs, his theory will remain squarely in the realm of fantasy and clickbait headlines.

ALIENS ARE RESPONSIBLE FOR CATTLE MUTILATIONS

Another colorful theory spread via pop culture, the concept of cattle mutilation is at once humorous and disturbing. The idea that aliens would cross the stars specifically to mess with our beef stock is, of course, ridiculous. But there are consistent stories among ranchers, going back to the 1970s, of cattle turning up dead with strange wounds.

These cases continue into the present day, as unsolved now as they were back then—just recently, in 2019, NPR's "All Things Considered"[20] covered a case of strange cattle mutilation in Oregon. And in some cases, UFOs have been sighted in the area prior to the mutilations. What does it all mean?

As with abductions, drawing any kind of correlation is a risky gamble, without proof. Best to keep our minds open, and your cattle secured. Maybe provide them with cow-sized tin foil hats, just in case.

So there you have it—some elements of UFO pop-culture match real UAP accounts, and others... not so much. As with many fringe sciences, UFOlogy is still riddled with myths, conjecture and incomplete theories. But unlike other fringe sciences, this one has been officially acknowledged by the U.S. government—and evidence indicates we've only scratched the surface of the enigma.

Wherever the unfolding saga of UAP disclosure takes us next, we can be sure of one thing: pop culture took us there first, and until we clear up these fanciful stories from our past, we cannot uncover the truths of the future.

---

20 NPR, " 'Not One Drop Of Blood': Cattle Mysteriously Mutilated In Oregon"

COVER ARTIST: KELLY WILLIAMS

KELLY WILLIAMS is a comic creator.

He mostly draws, sometimes writes, and always kills it. He's worked with publishers from Dark Horse to Satan himself—and just about everyone in between. (Not everyone though. That would be lying.)

He can be summoned to draw comics by playing jazz records backwards and hopping in a circle three times. He is a very serious person.

Planet Scumm conducted an interview with Kelly via email. Some text has been lightly edited for clarity.

PLANET SCUMM: Tell us a bit about the references that have inspired your art style over the years.

KELLY WILLIAMS: Most of my largest influences come from comics. I always come back to Bernie Wrightson as a big one but, I think, I kind of take a lot from anything that really grabs me. What am I feeling today? Maybe something more Jack Kirby or Brian Level?

The beautiful thing about art, in or outside of comics, is it never stops. There's always something new to find that will blow your mind. Always something or someone new to draw inspiration from. At one point, I really wanted to draw like Todd McFarland. Grew out of that (thankfully) pretty quickly and started focusing on figuring out how I draw.

It's obviously influenced by a little of everything I love, but I started to figure out how to be happier with my work once I figured out that I kinda have a "style."

PS: What is it that drew you towards working in comics?

KW: I guess largely, I've just always been into comics. Back to Wrightson again, Bernie was the first artist that I stopped and thought about, "Oh... there are people making these!"

It kinda blew my little kid brain to figure out that people had a job making comics. As I got a little older I really started wanting to make stories. So when I was around 13 or 14 (I think), I started making my own comics and xeroxing them. Just cheap photocopied mini comics. I did that for a LONG time.

Telling stories through comics is such a unique thing. It still is, even after everything that's happened with movies and video games, etc. There are just things you can do with comics that are so very specific to comics. Of course, it comes with its own unique challenges as well but, part of the fun is figuring that all out. I'm also a pretty big believer in there's no wrong way to make a comic. Everyone has their own voice and sometimes collaborating and bringing all those voices together to tell a story is just the best.

PS: Pulp storytelling is plot-driven, punchy, and often larger than life. Do you find it difficult to visually translate that tone when illustrating a story like [cover story] "Reptilian Barbarian"?

KW: Well... no more than anything else? I mean, that's what I work with on a daily basis making comics. Translating written word and breaking down visual representation of a scene in an effective, interesting way is what I do!

It's definitely not easy all the time. Even more so when you're having to give full sense of a scene in a single image. What's the really important stuff that needs to be there to say what's happening? What's the mood? Will people understand what's happening?

I guess it's most difficult when there is a ton of information that needs to be put in there while also being economic with how you show it and use the space. Pulp, much like horror (which I do a lot of) has unique visual challenges to try and hit the right spot to give you emotion or vibe or whatever.

When it comes to breaking something down to a single illustration, something like *Reptilian Barbarian* gives a lot of visual information so that always makes it a little easier to figure out.

PS: We've talked a bit about how you like to work between both physical and

digital mediums. Tell us about your art process and how a piece like your *Planet Scumm* cover comes together.

KW: Most everything I do is traditional. I just have a hard time moving away from physical medium because I like the tangibility of it, you know?

I generally do layouts or pencils digitally and then print them out at size. Depending on how clean I went, I'll sometimes just print the pencils lightly on the page and ink or paint right over it. Other times (probably most of the time), I'll flip it and print the roughs on the back of the page and lightbox it so I can see it through the paper and ink that way. I also tend to do ink and watercolor (or ink wash) on just about everything.

I'll sometimes color digitally but I'm not quite as good at adapting my overall coloring style to digital. Which is fine. I color differently when I do digital, and I like how it works when I do it. It's generally pretty simple. This one I did for *Scumm* is a good example of using a little of everything. I penciled digitally, printed and light boxed it to ink, added gray washes, scanned it and then colored it digitally.

PS: Where else can Scumm fans find you? Is there anything you're working on now that we can pick up or keep an eye out for?

KW: I'm working on a few new projects at the moment. The most recent new things out in the wild though are *The Life and*

Stage 1:
◄.... Thumbnail

Stage 2:
◄....... Pencils

Stage 3:
◄.........Inks

Death of the Brave Captain Suave, Issue 1, which is out from Scout Comics, *Yard Gang* is coming out from Storm King, and the *Razorblades* hardcover collection from Image comics has a story I drew. Those are the most recent things, not including covers and yadda yadda. I stay pretty busy for the most part.

FIND MORE FROM KELLY WILLIAMS:

» on twitter at @treebeerd
» on instagram at @treebeerdy
» website (updated about once a year...) at treebeerdstuff.com.

SPOT ILLUSTRATIONS

MAURA "MOE" McGONAGLE is a comic artist and illustrator, in addition to being *Planet Scumm's* rockstar production artist.

IN THIS ISSUE, MAURA'S ART CAN BE FOUND:

» *Title Page,*
» *Come the Banshee,* pg. 1
» *All Our Missing Pieces,* pg. 20
» *Reptilian Barbarian...,* pg. 55
» *Being Emily Was Too Hard,* pg. 66
» *A Collection of Endings,* pg. 73

JORDAN ALARCON is a studious aspiring character designer and digital painter.

IN THIS ISSUE, JORDAN'S ART CAN BE FOUND:

» *Single Malt Spacecraft,* pg. 11
» *The Pulse of Memory,* pg. 34
» *Burrowing Machines,* pg. 46

SAM RHEAUME is an illustrator-slash-graphic designer who operates in perpetual motion. He originated the visual style for *Planet Scumm's* black and gray spot illustrations.

IN THIS ISSUE, SAM'S ART CAN BE FOUND:

» *Pharinexin,* pg. 23
» *The Gardener,* pg. 26

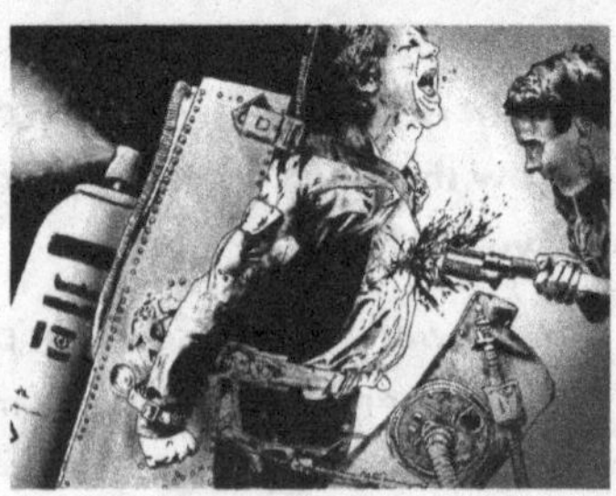

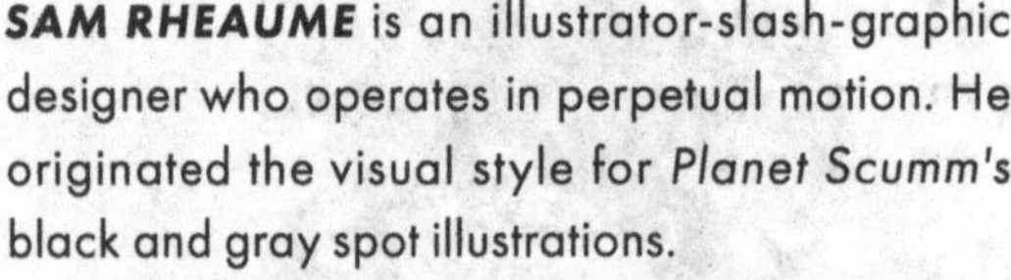

ADOPT A SLIMELING

What's a Slimeling, you ask? With a bit of coaxing—and a monthly contribution of a mere $3—anyone can befriend a slimeling.

These squishy companions are dangerously adorable and once you have one, you'll want more. They self-propogate and roam in packs—good news if you find yourself in need of highly-trainable guard/attack "dogs." (Keep that in mind when thoughts of invasion or mutiny creep into that head of yours.)

SIGN UP FOR THE $3 "SLIMELING" TIER ON OUR PATREON AND YOU'LL ENJOY:

» A digital book subscription. Get each new ebook on the day of release.

» Early access to *Planet Scumm* music and production updates on upcoming audio projects.

» Access to exclusive art prints, postcards, and/or stickers.

» $5 off at the *Planet Scumm* store.

» Invitation to *Scumm's* Author/Artist Discord, where we hold our writer's workshop.

» Other Scummy swag rocketing your way on a semi-regular basis.

» Plus, you get to practice your aim as you throw sustenance into the gaping maw of our indie publishing machine (from a safe distance).

ONCE MORE FOR EMPHASIS—
VISIT PLANETSCUMM ON PATREON FOR ALL YOUR SCI-FI AND SLIME-BUY NEEDS.

And when you're done there, take a look in the mirror. 'Cause those slimelings I just told you about? *They're behind you, and they might be your new best friend.*

EVERYTHING! VOLUME 2 IS STARTING ITS ENGINES

At last transmission, we relayed that *"Everything! Volume 2"* was well on its way towards aggregation—and good news, everyone! We have successfully managed to contain all that sci-fi goodness within the allotted rectangular constraints. *Hardcover* constraints, to be exact. Paperback just wouldn't do for a collection of this magnetude.

This holiday season, all 400+ pages of *"Everything! Volume 2"* will come crash-landing like an asteroid into your life, providing you with an inarguably superior format for *Planet Scumm Issues #5–10*. We humbly suggest that you keep your eyes glued to the screen because pre-orders will be coming this Winter to a web browser near you.